Paid to Take Control

Delphic Agency Book One

Romilly King

GW00472154

PAID TO TAKE CONTROL

First edition. December 1, 2022.

Copyright © 2022 Romilly King.

ISBN: 979-8215471548

Written by Romilly King.

Prologue

Of all the agencies in the USA, Delphic is the best. We have the most repeat Emptores buying their pleasure, and the most loyal Venditores earning good money from their most personal asset. Our contract success rate is 93%.

Nobody sells sex better than us. We're legal, we're ethical, and we pride ourselves on upholding not just the letter of the law but the spirit of it. We're here to make sure that the people who choose to sell sex, for whatever reason, don't get exploited.

We've been doing this for nearly twenty years now, ever since that last great depression, the one that followed all the pandemics, brought economies around the world to their knees. In the aftermath, the rich who had stayed rich took what they wanted for a tin of beans from those who had nothing.

Not happening, we the people said, so we regulated food and sex, and in the whirlwind of legislation around that, the Agencies were born to oversee and hold safe the contracts between those who sell sex and those who buy it.

Here at Delphic, we have a secret weapon - an algorithm that allows us to map the unconscious kinks and desires of the Venditores on our books and the Emptores who want to buy their services. It means we hit the gold standard of any business; we give the customer more than they knew they wanted.

We keep it very quiet because industrial espionage is a thing, and this is our edge.

The algorithm was developed a decade ago by a couple of guys out of MIT. It's incredible what can happen when you throw a genius neural biologist submissive and a dominant computer expert, who aren't remotely kink compatible, together at a time of their lives when their hormones are going bananas. They can generate amazing ideas in the pursuit of perfect pleasure!

It's a shame though, that genius submissive hasn't benefitted from the software he developed. We just couldn't track down the right match for him. And that sucked because he was one of the few who really suffered because of his needs, caught in the mental health whirlpool of his unfulfilled sexuality.

His needs were complex. He was submissive, bratty, masochistic, incredibly intelligent, driven in his work, and desperate in his desires. When it periodically all got too much for him, he turned to shady BDSM clubs, glory holes, gangbangs, and every mutation of unsafe sex he could lay himself in front of until he broke.

Eventually, his business partner decided enough was enough. Deliriously happy in his own relationship, Ash wanted the same for Brio, and if he couldn't find a match, then he would make a match.

This is Brio's story, just one of the many I have.

Chapter One

Brio the unicorn and the gloryhole

There were days when he couldn't cope. When everything felt swollen, soft, and rotten, like his skin was splitting open and his insides were spilling out. Days when he was so on edge that someone chewing with their mouth open sounded like an army of vaginas marching through mud, and he just wanted to kill them. Today had been one of those days, and it hadn't ended well.

Brio leaned back against the institutional green wall and adjusted his body language to display calm and collected. It would have worked better if half the guys in here hadn't seen him on his knees sucking off a line of cocks.

The knees of his jeans were damp with god knows what, and the skin beneath them was raw from kneeling. They hurt, with a dull ache, abrasions compounding pressure pain. Brio knew all about pain, but he didn't like this pain in these circumstances.

But he wanted more pain. He needed more pain.

His jaw ached, his head was sore from having his hair pulled, and his asshole throbbed because he had let an impatient guy fuck him when he didn't want to wait in line for his mouth.

Delicately, Brio took a fold on the inside of his swollen lower lip and nipped it. The sharp sting of it helped ground him as he started to drift down into images of hot flesh and cruel words.

Ash would be here soon. Ash and Richard were coming for him; he just had to hold on a little longer.

The holding cell wasn't rammed, but there were still ten other guys in here with Brio. It was a Thursday night, the night the guys who had regular fun things to do on Friday and Saturday evenings slid out quietly to do the bad stuff they never joked about with their friends.

3

Thursday night was lowlife sex night. It was why the cops had raided the glory hole at the back of the sex shop and why Brio was now in a holding cell. What he had been doing wasn't illegal – nobody paid him to get on his knees to suck off strangers – but the cops didn't know that, plus, resisting arrest was illegal. Brio had resisted, with his teeth.

A large guy in leather jeans and a stained t-shirt sidled up to Brio. "Gonna be a long night, pretty boy; Want to bump me to the head of the line while we're waiting?" When he raised his arm to lean flirtatiously against the wall, the waft of stale body odor made Brio jerk his head back. Inside his head, the submissive mewled, begged, and scratched at the frayed mental ropes Brio had wrapped around him. He wanted, needed more. To be held down and fucked. Passed around until he was nothing but a live wire connection of nerves between one man's desire and the next. Taken until he floated free and could never find his way back.

"Fuck off." Brio didn't waste an explanation on the guy; he didn't have it in him. Right now, he was holding on to reality by the skin of his teeth.

"You sure? You looked like you were really enjoying what you were getting before." The guy leaned closer and whispered in Brio's ear, "I got a real thick cock, it would look perfect stretching those pretty lips of yours, and I don't mind giving a show to these guys."

The guy's eyes were dark with lust, and everyone in the holding cell was watching them. It sent his nerves jangling with the desire to be good, to give them what they wanted, to reach for the promise of that floating, peaceful, brain calming quiet of submission.

His knees trembled, yearning to bend.

"Yeah, you'd get on your knees for me, wouldn't you, pretty boy?" The guy's voice was heavy with the promise of debasement. Brio couldn't hold on; he was going to go down.

Loud metal clanged as the door to the holding cells opened. Brio dragged his eyes away from the man next to him.

Through the bars, he saw Ash. The lock of his gaze was a lifeline thrown into the dirty flash flood inside Brio's head.

The guy stepped away as the police officer opened the holding cell door.

"You," he nodded at Brio, "you're bailed. Time to get the fuck out of here."

Ash wore faded jeans and his ancient MIT hoody with his hands shoved into the center pocket. With mussed hair and rumpled clothes, he looked as if he'd just rolled out of bed, which given the time of night he obviously had. His skin was darkly tanned from his honeymoon, but he squinted with tiredness; jumping time zones was a bitch. Behind him, Brio could see Richard. Naturally, Richard was more put together than Ash. His nice button-up under a casual jacket and navy blue pants made him look more like a duty lawyer than an academic.

Brio pushed himself off the wall and moved towards Ash. He knew his steps faltered because each one caused the humiliation to build. By the time he stood in front of his partner, his eyes were prickling. *Here comes the drop.*

Ash quirked a smile, but it trembled at the corners. "What's the story, Morning Glory?" he whispered.

Tears overflowed from Brio's eyes, tracking down his cheeks. "Usual tale, Nightingale." He shrugged with all the sorrow inside him.

"I know, but this time we're going to get it sorted, I swear."

Richard moved forward, his long arm wrapping around Brio's shoulder. "Come on," he said softly. "Come with me. Ash is going to sort the paperwork."

Brio let himself be lead out of the door. Behind him, leather pants guy complained about his blow job being aborted for the second time.

"I'll catch you next time, pretty boy," he yelled. "Going to be real sweet for the waiting."

"Over my dead body," Richard muttered.

Brio hung his head in shame, letting the feeling take up residence inside him yet again.

Brio stood with Richard while Ash filled in release paperwork, paid over bail money, and charmed the ass off the custody officers. If he was lucky, he could get away with a slap on the wrist for this, and Ash would make sure he was lucky.

More sorrow and guilt swelled in Brio. It was always him causing shit for Ash. Loyal, smart, loving Ash – he didn't need the crap Brio brought, particularly now, just when everything was going right for him. Hell, he couldn't have been home from his honeymoon for more than a couple of hours when Brio had used his one phone call to dump his problems on Ash again.

Brio slumped, and Richard's strong arm around his shoulders held him up. Brio liked Richard, he had a sly, dry humor that Brio adored, but he didn't really get him and Ash.

Ash was a Dominant through and through, from his walk to his expression, and Richard was, well Richard was stoic and professional, and yeah he looked hot, but he looked normal – Brio could never hide what he was, he didn't have it in him, his vibe had always been that little bit off – but Richard, never in a million years would he have put him and Ash together. Clearly, their algorithm was better than he thought because it spat Richard out, and Ash had been head over heels for him since the moment they met.

"I can't stop," Ash had told him once, "I look at him, and I know he will do anything for me, just me, nobody else, and I have to have him and keep making him look like that."

Brio couldn't imagine Richard writhing in ecstasy or begging, but Ash, drunk off his tits one night in LA, confessed that Richard liked to be cock caged, and he liked to be denied, and when Ash tied him he sank into subspace so fast it was like a comet dropping.

Brio had shivered with jealousy at that, not because he wanted Ash in that way, but because he wanted what he and Richard had - that duality, that dynamic that matched. He had had to go blow a random bear in the bathroom after Ash had said that, just to take the edge off, and when he came back, Ash had been pissed with him.

Ash was often pissed with him. Right now, despite his calm exterior and natural charm, making the police officers laugh, Brio knew Ash was angry, angry and scared, and that was never a good combination in a dominant. Brio assumed he was really in for it this time.

Not that he didn't deserve it. This time he had gone too far. But the itch under his skin, the need, the flip flop of his desires, it grew stronger every month, and he didn't know where to go from here.

College had been his most stable time, and even then there had been "episodes". Episodes were what Brio chose to call his periodic descents into sexual degradation. Without Ash Brio knew he wouldn't have made anything of himself. Being brilliant wasn't all it was cracked up to be, in his opinion - if you paired genius with a personality as unfortunate as his, there were too many pitfalls to navigate between potential and success.

Ash was his rock. Ash was his lifeline. Ash was his friend, and he loved him with his whole heart. If he and Ash had been sexually compatible, Brio was pretty sure he would have a Nobel Prize by now!

Thrown together that first day at MIT snarky and opinionated Brio had been paired with driven and surprisingly shy Ash, and each had found their best friend. Brio made Ash more outgoing and dragged him away from his deep dives into math and probability. Ash made Brio feel normal and less like an alien studying the bizarre ways of humanity.

The day Ash found out about Brio's secret was the foundation stone their long relationship was built on. Stressed to his limit by the relentless pressure of a double master's program, Brio had taken himself to a shady BDSM club and gotten himself beaten bloody with a single tail and double teamed by a pair of lousy doms who high fived each other over his body.

He had dragged himself back to his dorm in full sub drop, and when he fell through the door, face streaked with tears and shirt stuck to his back with blood, Ash had done precisely the opposite of what Brio had expected.

Ash had held him, cleaned him up, and cuddled him, told him he was good and stayed wrapped around him throughout the night. The next morning when Brio woke up Ash had been lying beside him, reading a textbook, Ash had smiled down at him with genuine affection, "What's the story, Morning Glory?" he had asked.

"Usual tale, Nightingale," Brio had replied, then he told Ash about his history of sexual extremes.

Ash had put safety measures in place. A systems man to the tips of his fingers, Ash believed Brio's problems could be managed with the right protocols. And to a degree, they could. For years, they sort of worked, but the older he got, the worse his "episodes" became. Now, Brio had to admit to himself that the risks he took were getting more extreme. If he didn't end up as a depraved millionaire headline on the gossip sites, he would end up severely injured, perhaps dead.

Brio shivered in the pre-dawn chill as they left the police station. Richard slipped off his jacket and carefully wrapped Brio in it. He managed a half-grin for his partner's husband.

"I need you to take this Bri." Ash held out a small pill, and Brio reached obediently for it.

"Is it okay to give him anything?" Richard asked. "What if he has taken something?"

"He never takes drugs."

Brio put the pill in his mouth and let it dissolve on his tongue with the familiar quick to paste, bitter taste of diazepam.

"Do we need to take him to a doctor? I could call Cash..."

"No, we'll just take him home, clean him up, get him settled, he's going to be staying with us for a few weeks."

Brio blinked at Ash. "No," he managed to get the word out.

"Yes." Ash wasn't angry, but there was an adamant quality about him, the dominant that had matured over the years and finally flowered with Richard, front and center. Brio felt it vibrate inside him, all delicious clarity and surety.

He dropped his eyes, "Okay," he hung his head, "I'm sorry,"

"You're not sorry, Brio," Ash said, his voice unhappy. "You're sorry for the hassle, but you're not sorry for what you did, and that's okay, but we're gonna find a safer way for you to get what you need." He reached out and cupped Brio's face. "I love you. You're my partner, we created something together that makes people happier, and that's awesome. Now it's your time, brother; this ends here. You deserve so much more than this."

Brio swallowed the sob that tried to escape from his throat and tried to dredge up a "Fucking, yeah!" grin for Ash, but it was a poor attempt.

It was good enough to be rewarded with Ash's sweet, half quirked smile. "Get in the car, Brio," Ash said, "Try and sleep. It'll take about an hour to get home."

Brio clambered into the back seat and lay down. He curled his long body into itself and waited for the drugs to pull a blanket over his twitching, itching brain.

He was aware when the car started, and Ash maneuvered out of the parking garage, he let the sound of the wheels lull him, and he closed his eyes.

"You never did explain to me why you call him a unicorn." Richard's voice was quiet, but Brio could hear it clearly over the road noise, "You call him a unicorn and say things like he's 'out there in terms of his needs'" Brio imagined the air quotes that Richard had applied to the comment, "But you've never given specifics and now we've picked him up from a holding cell after he got arrested for biting a police officer when they raided a glory hole where he was clearly the main attraction."

Brio couldn't hear any censor in Richard's voice, just concern. He would have preferred censor. Judgment he understood, judgment he could live with, concern implied that his choices were poor because there were alternatives he could have taken.

Ash gave a low laugh. "I call him a unicorn because he's everybody's fantasy. He's super bright, pretty, and kinky as fuck. He's what every Dom dreams of having. But the thing with unicorns, if you think about them logically, is that they are half a ton of stomp you to pieces animal with a massive horn in the middle of their forehead. Fantasy wise they are awesome; the reality can be a whole lot scarier.

"Brio takes no prisoners if he's not getting what he needs, and he's a fucking neural biologist who can turn your brain inside out within seconds. He will spot your pressure point and ram his thumb in it until you scream. So yeah, cute fantasy animal, not so much!"

"And the 'out there' needs?" Richard prompted.

"He's an extreme submissive, as you know," Ash said. Brio could hear Ash's fingers drumming on the steering wheel. "But more than that, his needs change day to day; he is like a multiple personality disorder of kink. As a baseline, he needs domestic discipline. If he's deep into research, he needs to be reminded to eat, exercise, and sleep: a daily spanking seemed to help him with that at one point.

"But that is not the sum total of his kinks. On any given day, Brio could need anything from pain and impact play, edging with no chance of orgasm, complex shibari, hand feeding and vanilla sex, or pet play. All these things fulfill some particular portion of his psyche, but there is no telling when each area will activate next. All we know is that not having those needs met leads to nights like this. He goes out and puts himself in the way of as much sexual degradation as he can find. And trust me, when you look like he does, that's pretty easy to find."

"Why not just hire several Doms to meet Brio's various needs?" Richard suggested.

"Tried that," said Ash. "At one point, we had a rotating team on speed dial. It didn't work because he doesn't know what he needs until he needs it."

"So what we need is a psychic Venditor," mused Richard. "who not only shares these kinks but can form a connection with Brio strong enough to anticipate them?"

"That would be an option, but it's practically impossible to arrange. Safe scenes require planning, and Brio won't wait around while some professional Dom flips through their playbook."

They were both silent for a moment, then Richard asked, "Did the new version of the algorithm throw up any possibilities at Delphic?"

"One." Brio could almost hear the eye roll in Ash's voice. "Ms. Sara threw a fucking fit when I approached her about him. Said she'd offered specialist contracts to the guy before, but he only took one-off vanilla contracts and was the laziest Venditor they had on the books. She would have kicked him in to touch years ago, but in the ten years he's been a Venditor, he's barely been out of a contract because he has the highest possible satisfaction ratings."

"Really?" Brio stifled a smile at the irony in Richard's tone. "Why don't you replay what you just said and run it through that massive data crunching brain of yours? See if you can drag something useful out of it."

Brio could only imagine the glare Ash would be shooting his husband, but there was a moment's silence as Ash did what Richard suggested.

"Fuck," Ash breathed, "cognitive dissonance towards his Dom persona. He has a Dom inside him, the algorithm can see it, but he can't or won't acknowledge it. Being lazy would normally kill him in the satisfaction stakes, but he must have a high empathy rating to give the Emptores exactly what they want. I bet the satisfaction he gets from the caretaker part of being a Venditor is enough to keep his Dom persona quiet if not fully satisfied."

"There you go." Richard sounded smug. "You're not just a pretty face, are you?"

"And you are going into chastity for two weeks," Ash said brightly.

"It still doesn't solve the problem, though," Richard replied, not as smug as he'd been. "The guy is just a potential match on paper. He has no experience and an obvious mental block on his kinks. On a side note, Brio hasn't consented to anything."

"You were just a potential match on paper," Ash pointed out.

Score for Ash, Brio thought sleepily.

"And I did say if we couldn't find Brio a Dom, I'd make one for him," Ash added.

"Yeah, and that's bound to go well," Richard muttered, but he must have said it quietly because Ash would have upped his chastity punishment if he'd heard.

Brio smirked. The drugs were kicking in, and the itch under his skin had faded away, leaving just soreness. The road noise had become a thrumming lullaby. He tucked his hands between his thighs and curled up tighter. He imagined the Dom Ash would make for him. He wanted a nice one, one with a heavy hand and a hug that wrapped around him like a soft blanket, a rope man with patience and nimble fingers who would praise Brio while he hurt him. Brio sighed and slipped into sleep.

Chapter Two

Painter and the boyfriend experience

Hiding his hangover behind full mirrored Raybans, Painter cautiously walked along the long corridor to psych evaluation. His head hurt so badly that his usual loping stride might have made him throw up. Resting his forehead against the wall, he peered over his glasses and keyed his personal code into the door's control panel. He slid into the room before slumping into the seat before the familiar screen.

"Good morning, Painter." The AI had a pleasant male voice. "Please, remove your sunglasses and insert your whole hand into the glove." Painter blinked; the AI sounded different. If he didn't know better, it sounded a bit saucy.

"What the hell," Painter muttered, "another upgrade." He slipped his glasses into his top pocket and put his right hand and wrist into the glove attachment on the chair, wriggling his fingers to settle them against the sensor pads. The glove blinked LEDs three times, then the grip on his wrist tightened against his pulse.

Painter yawned and settled in the chair, stretching out his long legs and blinked tiredly. Surely, he didn't need to go through psych eval again? He'd had one three weeks ago, along with his full annual physical and mental check-up, just before his last contract. He didn't know why he needed an additional AI exam now. But this was the Delphic Agency, they prided themselves on being the best, and if they wanted another test, he sat another test and didn't moan about it.

Take the line of least resistance, that was Painter's motto, no point in rocking any boats.

The lights in the small room dimmed, a low-level color sequence danced around the perimeter, red chased green, yellow chased blue.

14

"Just relax," murmured the AI. "Just watch the screen, sir, and let me take care of you."

That's odd, Painter thought as the screen in front of him pulsed, and the images began flickering faster than the naked eye could grasp. *It's never called me sir before.*

Two days later, Painter was back at Delphic for a meeting with Ms. Sara.

"Hey, gorgeous." Painter smirked at her in the way he knew drove her crazy as he strolled into her bright sunny office and threw himself into a chair. "What ya got for me? Who needs the boyfriend experience next?"

Ms. Sara glared at him then raised one perfect eyebrow. "Jeans, Painter? Is your suit at the dry cleaners?"

"We've known each other long enough." Painter winked at her, just as a reminder of years gone by. "We don't need to play formal after all this time, do we?" He threw a long leg over the arm of the chair and grinned obnoxiously. Driving Ms. Sara nuts was one of the highlights of his job.

"It would have been helpful if you had dressed appropriately today, Painter." She sighed and shuffled folders on her desk. "We have a meeting with an Emptor's representative shortly; we have a specialist contract we'd like to offer you."

"I don't do specialist contracts," Painter said easily; this was an old familiar argument. "You know the score, Sara, in and out, boyfriend experiences, short, sweet, vanilla, and never the same one twice."

"I appreciate that, Painter. God knows I've been dealing with your contracts for long enough, but I'm afraid I'm going to need to insist that you consider this, particularly given your most recent psych eval.

"The new software upgrade has reassessed your scores, and you are now showing as aggressively sexually dominant; we can't offer you vanilla contracts anymore, you're a risk."

What the fuck? The smirk vanished from Painter's face. He placed his feet back on the floor and leaned forward. "What the hell Sara? You've known me for a decade; I'm no dominant, I don't do kink at all!"

"Your markers say you are a high-level dominant."

"My markers can go fuck themselves," Painter said pleasantly. "I've been offered these contracts in the past, and they are truly not my thing."

"Think of it as a career progression." Ms. Sara was trying to sell this, and Painter didn't understand why. The energy from her was excessive, stressed and desperate. Their regular interactions were baiting and bitchy, not this intense.

"There will be training, full training. We'd never let you go in unprepared; we value our Venditores. And then there's the increased pay. Contracts like this one fall outside of government pay scales, so the remuneration will be twice your normal rate."

Painter stared at her, trying to work out the angle here.

"If it turns out, down the line, that you aren't fully comfortable with kink contracts, then you could switch to training. Once you had the requisite experience, you could get out of fieldwork, chill out, kick back, have a steady salary."

Painter narrowed his eyes; there was a desperation about this that set off all his alarm bells.

"I think there must be some mistake," he said, trying to keep his tone even. "I know Delphic have suggested kink contracts for me in the past, but turning them down has never been a problem. I'm a nice guy, Sara. Okay, I'm a little lazy and laid back, and I have sex for money, but everyone leaves happy; nobody gets hurt."

Painter was very aware that being a nice guy was pretty much all he had going for him. He fell into working for Delphic straight out of college to pay off student loans on his pointless degree – Marine biology - who knew how few jobs that qualified you for? Venditor work turned out to be comfortable and profitable, and he never got around to formulating an exit strategy. He wasn't interested in career progression though, and he sure as hell wasn't going to get a proper job with his resume, but to go into a contract where he hurt people for money? No way, that wasn't nice!

"I can't hurt someone," he stated bluntly.

"I think you'll find you probably can once you feel the results," Ms. Sara replied, her voice bland, her tone level, but her eyes hinted at something he didn't understand. *Was that disgust?*

"Consent goes both ways; that's how we work." Anger bubbled, and that was an emotion he had suppressed for years. *Never get angry, never get aggressive.* "Why are you trying to force me into this?"

"Because you are bloody lying to yourself. You know you want this, and you are pretending otherwise."

Painter looked up, shocked.

"Look at your test results." Ms. Sara leaned forward and slid a folder across the desk. "See where you are on the dominance graph and then read the report." She sighed and settled back into her chair as Painter reluctantly pulled the paperwork towards himself.

"I am all about consent, Painter. I always have been. And I am not forcing you to do this." She used both hands to push tiny strands of hair that had escaped her hairstyle back up from her forehead. "But even if you don't take this particular contract, I can't let you take any more vanilla contracts based on these results. It wouldn't be right for you, and it could lead to an adverse outcome with an Emptor."

"So if I don't do this, you're cutting me loose?" His stomach churned. This was all he was good for; he didn't know what else to do if he wasn't fucking for money.

"Read the fucking report, Painter," Ms. Sara sighed wearily, "then I'll explain your options."

Painter scanned the report. Phrases jumped out at him randomly.

Sadism – 85th percentile

Dominant – 97th percentile

Kinks identified as bondage - including predicament – and heavy impact play.

With every additional damning word, he became more lightheaded. He felt naked. *Exposed.*

He looked up from the treacherous report when a tall man entered the room with only the briefest of knocks and settled himself in a chair as if he owned the place.

"Painter, this is Mr. Ash Gannon," Ms. Sara said. "He works with us on technology development. He is also the representative of the Emptor we would like to offer your services to."

Painter glanced at him, taking in the tailored suit, the handmade shoes, and the air of significant money that, as an experienced Venditor, he could sniff out a mile away.

"I'm afraid there has been a mistake," Painter said. "There must have been a glitch in the system or something because I don't do specialist contracts."

"There are no glitches in my systems." The man's voice was even, but his eyes raked over Painter, assessing him, logging everything.

Painter reined in the dark aggression that simmered inside him and dragged out his winning smile. "Well honestly, Mr. Gannon, if you have someone who matches this–" he placed his damning report on the desk, "–they don't need a Venditor, they need a therapist."

"I think you should take the information in the report on board," Ms. Sara said. "Your markers for sexual dominance have been increasing over the years. You've always turned down BDSM and kink contracts, but it seems that you would be perfect for them." Her tone was placating, and it pissed Painter off.

"This isn't me." Painter slammed his hand down on the report, "This is not who I am!"

"Oh, I really fucking think it is." Ash Gannon's voice was calm, unyielding. "It takes one to know one." He turned to Ms. Sara. "Painter and I are going to go and have a private discussion; I'll speak to you later."

Ms. Sara nodded sharply. Painter was astonished at her easy acceptance of Gannon's order. *Who is this guy?*

Ash stood; he shook his cuffs and rolled his shoulders as if to release tension. "Come with me," he said and didn't look to see if Painter was behind him as he left the room.

Painter followed Ash down one of the Agency's endless pale green corridors. Gannon paused and knocked briefly on a nondescript door, and without waiting for an answer, opened it and stuck his head inside. "I need you to join me in Conference Room Three. Can you bring Brio's file and his latest compatible charter? Great, thanks." He closed the door and without explaining himself, strode on. Painter trailed behind him feeling off-center and irritated.

Conference Room Three turned out to be an unexpectedly sunny room. Wide windows overlooked the tranquil lake that was the centerpiece of the Agency grounds. On the whiteboard that took up a third of one wall, someone had scrawled a bullet point list of pre-contract assessment criteria. Ash looked at it and snorted in amusement.

"Sit," he said to Painter and scratched irritably at the designer scruff on his cheeks.

Painter glared at him but took a seat, crossed one long leg over the other, and attempted to appear nonchalant. Gannon silently paced back and forth in front of the window as they waited for whoever the fuck it was that had also been ordered to come here.

Painter ignored the uncomfortable silence that Gannon allowed to build.

He ostentatiously pulled his phone out, and less obviously, ran a search for Ash Gannon. Know thy enemy and all that.

It turned out Ash Gannon was an expert in computer algorithms and co-founder of ManMindMaps, the team compatibility software. Even Painter had heard of 3M – he remembered some Football team hitting the headlines a few years ago when they sacked their entire squad, rebuilt a new team from cheaper players, and then won the European League.

He'd read an article about it while on a yacht in the Aegean. He had been on contract for a wealthy fashion designer, and he had been restless one night, suffering from his periodic insomnia, and had spent the night reading anything dull enough to put him to sleep. The Football team had put their success down exclusively to the team compatibility software ManMindMaps had built for them.

Wikipedia didn't explain why a computer expert would be stamping around Delphic like he owned the place.

A memory flickered and fell loose from a stack in the back of Painter's head. That Aegean contract had been shitty. He hadn't liked the fashion designer, but the real reason he couldn't sleep that night had been because of how his skin itched, and his mind refused to settle after he fucked his Emptor into a deep, dreamless sleep.

He remembered the thought that had crossed his mind when he read the article - *shame we don't use this shit at Delphic, then I wouldn't get matched to guys who do nothing for me. This gig would be way more fun if we all wanted each other.*

Fuck, things started to fall into place.

The changing psych tests over the years.

The kink contracts they repeatedly offered, that he always turned down.

The bullshit psych report he'd just read.

He looked up to see the other man staring at him. "And there it is," Gannon said snarkily. "The light dawns."

The door to the room opened, and a tousle-haired man with black glasses entered. He had a laptop bag slung over his shoulder and carried a folder in the standard Delphic pink for Emptores. He wore suit pants and an open-collared white shirt with the tie dragged loose and low, and the sleeves rolled up. "Sorry," he muttered, "I had to log out of the system, and I was in deep."

Gannon stepped forward, and Painter rose to his feet. Gannon took the folder from the other man and slung it on the small conference table. "Thanks for coming; I'm having trouble getting through to this one," he said.

Painter was getting increasingly pissed. He felt very much out of his depth at this point. Between being offered an uncomfortable contract, and a psych report that laid out exactly how deviant he would be if he ever let out the shadow brother in his brain, he'd just about had enough for one day.

"I'll just set up here then." The new arrival flashed Painter a shy smile and glanced at him over his glasses with pretty green eyes.

"This is Painter," Gannon told him. "Painter, this is Cashel."

"And who the fuck is Cashel, Superman's cousin?"

The other man rolled his eyes. "Not the first time I've heard that." he smiled. "I'm Dr. Cashel Gregory, head of Delphic's Clinical Psychology Department. I liaise between the Agency and Ash's organization, and I also work with Venditores and Emptors who need me. In this instance, I am here in my professional capacity to assist with overseeing the mental health needs of a complex contract."

Painter was surprised that this unassuming young man held such a prominent position, but then he supposed some people didn't take the road he had chosen and did better for themselves as a result. He shrugged off the mental stings his profession wanted to at jab him; it could be worse.

"Sorry, Doc," he said. "It's been a weird day."

Dr. Cashel nodded. "I'm sure it has, and maybe Ash has been less than diplomatic because this is so important to him."

It was Gannon's turn to roll his eyes. "Guy's not listening to anybody."

"It's not compulsory," the doctor said gently.

"It's getting that way," Gannon replied, profound sorrow apparent in his voice.

That tone of voice had more impact on Painter than anything he had heard so far. He took a seat at the conference table. "Look, I'm sorry, but this has been a lot to take in. Do you want to start at the beginning and tell me the story?"

"Morning glory," Gannon whispered to himself before he cleared his throat, embarrassed.

"Right." Dr. Gregory sat down. "Let me summarise the situation as it appears to me – I have spoken to Ms. Sara, so I am up to speed." He paused for a moment as if to gather his thoughts. "Normally, we try to be as anonymous as possible during contract negotiations. But in certain instances, we have to get specific because arrangements are complex, peculiar, or particularly sensitive. This is one of those situations.

"The contract Ms. Sara wanted you to consider was to take on the role of professional Dominant to a sexually submissive man called Brio." He held up his hand to forestall Painter's immediate refusal. "I know you don't want the contract, but please listen a little longer.

"Brio is a complex man; he is highly intelligent and extremely motivated in his work. He also has submissive needs so complex that if they are not met, they result in behavior that puts both his mental and physical health at severe risk."

Painter glanced over at Gannon, wondering what about the connection – brother, maybe?

"As you're clearly curious, he's my business partner," Ash said. "He's the co-founder of triple M."

Well, that was surprising.

"Brio is what is known as a high-level submissive," Dr. Gregory continued. "He has a significant number of kinks, and he needs his submissive side exercising regularly to keep him stable and settled. Due to the variety of his kinks and the speed with which they overwhelm him, we have, to date, been unable to find a dominant to match him."

"Yeah, I'm afraid you've lost me, Doc. Who the fuck needs a specific kind of sex to keep them stable?"

"Pretty much everyone," Gannon deadpanned.

Painter laughed, but the laughter died when he saw the severe expressions on Gannon and Dr. Gregory's faces. "You aren't kidding?"

"No, we're not," Dr. Gregory said. "Please look in the file." He pushed it across the table towards Painter.

"People keep throwing bits of paper at me today and expecting me to accept what's written on them as gospel," Painter groused, but he opened the folder and scanned the document.

On the left was a headshot of a laughing dark-haired man with a wide smile and soulful brown eyes. His hair was shaggy, and he had a dimple in his left cheek. With his head tilted up, Painter could see the long line of his throat and his sharp chin. For some reason, the look on the guy's face made him quirk a smile. *Pretty, really pretty.*

On the right-hand page were his statistics: age, education, location rundown– *Jesus, a double doctorate* –. Halfway down the page was a bold type headline Kink Summary.

Highly Submissive – 95th percentile

Masochistic tendencies – 85th percentile

Kinks identified: shibari, impact play, restraint, chastity, edging, nonsexual age play, puppy play, control, and domination.

Venditor requirements: Brio requires a highly empathic Dominant with not only a wide-ranging skillset but the ability to deduce what he needs on any given day as his submissive presentation cycles through his kinks. The recommendation is for a long-term stable dominant (one-year minimum) with daily contact and regular weekends focussed on extended play play. Brio will only respond positively to a dominant with compatible kinks. His high empathy allows him to sense those who dom for pay and that compounds his low self-esteem. Plus, as a pronounced masochist, Brio requires a Dom who can revel in his pain and provide genuine aftercare. Without thorough aftercare, he drops badly and his issues spiral quickly.

Brio can be highly manipulative and challenging as a submissive but with the right partner, on the right day, he can drop easily into subspace. Incidents like this result in a more sustained up phase in his mood and mental health. It is my opinion that with a truly compatible dominant in a long-term contract, Brio could reach equilibrium with his submissive nature, and the wider benefits on his life and future would be profound.

Painter rubbed a finger between his eyebrows; he hadn't hit the bottom of the rabbit hole yet. He sighed. "So let me get this straight you guys think that I am a Dominant with kinks that match your man and if I agree to fuck him as he wants, he'll stop behaving like a dick."

"He doesn't just behave like a dick; he could fucking die," Gannon was on his feet. Dr. Gregory had a hand on his forearm, broadcasting calming vibes and encouraging Ash to sit back down, murmuring to him.

"Look, guys," Painter tried to be sensible, "I get that you are scientists and you have this crazy theory, but honestly, I've been a professional Venditor for ten years, and I can tell you that this isn't the way it works."

"That's true for most people," said Dr. Gregory. "But just like the Kinsey scale for sexuality, the kink scale doesn't matter much to most people. For the huge mass of people in the middle, they are what they are, they accept their nature, and their needs are met easily. But some people, those on the far ends of the scale, struggle.

"You can compare it to those who historically struggled with their homosexuality and gender – and Brio is one of those people on the far edge. Funnily enough, so are you, but you've found a way to subvert the demands of your inner dominant and you're coping better than he is."

Painter shook his head. "This is bullshit man; it doesn't work like that."

"We're getting nowhere with this," Gannon said. "Time to show and tell,"

Dr. Gregory sighed. "I'll set the laptop up."

"Don't bother," said Gannon and pulled his phone from his pocket. "He gets the adult version; I'm calling Ricky."

"I don't think that's appropriate, Ash."

"Tough," Gannon fiddled with his phone.

Dr. Gregory sighed and turned to Painter. "I would just ask you to try and keep an open mind. We'll just go through the graphs for a moment."

Painter was lost as soon as Dr. Gregory pulled up two neural mapping graphics on his computer and attempted to show him how they compared. One was his and the other belonged to this Brio guy.

He could see synchronicity between them, but it meant nothing to him; they were just brain shapes filled with flickering light nodes.

A few minutes later, the door to the conference room opened, and a tall, well-built man entered. He was extremely attractive, lithe and graceful with an intelligent, somber gaze. His expression was composed until he spotted Gannon and then a glorious smile broke across his face. Gannon rose and strode towards him. Painter realized that at that moment, there was nobody else in the room to Gannon, just this man. A shock of loneliness shivered through him, and he pressed it down ruthlessly.

"Baby." Gannon reached out and cupped the other man's face with almost unbearable sweetness. Painter swallowed, his mouth suddenly dry.

"They have that effect on people," Dr. Gregory whispered, and his gaze on Painter was knowing.

Taking the man's hand, Gannon pulled him forward. "This is Painter, the prospect. He's not getting with the program; please be kind enough to tell him who you are and what you do."

The man smiled at him, radiating calm confidence, "Hi, Painter, I've heard a lot about you. It's nice to meet you. I'm Richard Gannon, Ash's husband." He smiled at the man beside him. "I am currently enrolled in D.U. Graduate School where I am due–" he glanced at his watch, "–in 28 hrs. time to defend my DPhil on the rise of kink centric literature during the early years 21st century, after which, I will be Dr. Gannon."

Gannon smiled proudly at Richard. "Oh, and Ricky, what's your safeword?"

Richard turned to Gannon and quirked his head, then he smiled. "Vista," he said confidently.

"Kneel," said Gannon and Richard went gracefully to his knees.

Painter's cock got hard in microseconds, the traitorous fucker.

Watching Ash spank his husband was a revelation on so many different levels that Painter felt his worldview unraveling.

Firstly there was the intense sexual arousal that had him throbbing in his jeans as he watched Ash bend Richard over the conference room table, bare his ass and then proceed to deliver ten sharp cracks across it. The sound of the hand on flesh, Richard's bitten back whimpers, the humiliated flush on his face, and the fierce, possessive look on Ash's, all sang to him with a siren's song.

When Ash pulled Richard upright against him and murmured praises into his neck, Painter could see Richard's substantial erection sticking straight out in front of him. It looked delicious, but in the center of his soul, Painter thought it would be even more delicious if Richard was soft.

He closed his eyes and tried to push the dark desire under, the urge to take what was offered and drown in it, then push for more and more until the man he controlled gave up his very being.

When he opened his eyes again, Ash was looking at him over Richard's shoulder. One hand was around Richard's throat, holding him back to him; the other toyed lazily with Richard's erection.

"Oh, there you are," said Ash with a certain smugness. "Nice to finally meet you."

Painter realized he was breathing heavily. His hands were fisted on his thighs, as he leaned forward, his posture aggressive, and his cock was so hard he could have hammered nails with it.

Ash licked a stripe up Richard's neck, and Richard trembled in his grasp, his cock bobbing. "Bet you would like one of these," Ash taunted.

"That's enough, Ash," Dr. Gregory's voice was harsh. "Take Richard and look after him."

"Always," said Ash easily, but he turned Richard towards him, bent, pulled up his pants, then planted a soft kiss on Richard's mouth. "Love you, Ricky, you are amazing," he murmured. He led Richard out of the room with an arm wrapped around his waist. Painter noted how Richard leaned into Ash, and he itched to have that trust shown in him.

Dr. Gregory took his glasses off, polished them, then let out a slow breath and looked at Painter sideways. "How do you feel?" he asked.

"Do they teach you the exact right way to say that your first week in Psychologist school?" Painter snarked.

"I practiced in front of the mirror for months," replied Dr. Gregory. "Took me ages to get the caring tone right."

Painter hung his head and blew out a huff of laughter. "That was crazy," he said.

"Yeah, it was, but it worked, didn't it," Dr. Gregory's look was assessing, "It turned you on, a lot."

"Yep," Painter scrubbed his hands over his face, "like you wouldn't believe."

"Have you ever been around anything like that before?"

"Nope, not in real life."

"In porn?"

"Yeah, and in my head." Painter sighed. "Sometimes I get these fantasies when I've taken a break from contracts or if they are boring or..." He trailed off.

"Go on," Dr. Gregory encouraged.

"It's there, sure, I always knew it was, but I don't want it. I don't want to be that person, I want to be nice."

"You don't think you can be dominant and nice?"

"You think you can?"

"Actually, yes." Dr. Gregory turned to him, his gaze serious. "I think that some of the nicest people I know are dominants. They are caring, loyal, and determined. Ash is actually one of the nicest people I know. When he isn't worried sick or in that part of his persona, he is shy, sweet, and ridiculously dorky."

Painter rolled his eyes; he couldn't see that.

"I think the most sensible way forward is for you to take a few classes," Dr. Gregory said. "Don't dismiss the contract out of hand. Learn, consider, reflect, and then have a few meetings with Brio, and see if you resonate together. We have time.

"Ash is worried about Brio because he is protective of him, but Brio isn't a basket case, and after his latest drop, he has gotten it out of his system for a while. We can take our time with this, and you'll be paid while you are in contract negotiations and training. We can go at your pace."

Painter found himself nodding. "I'll give it a go. I guess I should at least take some courses because it looks like it's out of the box in my head now, and given the way I responded to that, I'm going to struggle to get it back in."

Dr. Gregory laughed. "Relax, it's not like you're never going to have vanilla sex again! Vanilla sex is great. Amazing; even kinky people have it more often than anything else. It's not like we always need to have our foot in a bear trap and be punched in the face to come!"

"That was weirdly specific, Doc." Painter raised his eyebrows at the psychologist.

Chapter Three

Brio and the reluctant dominant

"Is he late?" Brio asked. "I hate it when people are late; it makes me feel like I'm not worth turning up for."

"He's not late," said Cashel mildly and continued making notes in the margins of the report he was reading. They were sitting in the pleasant sunshine of the Agency gardens, close to the lake and away from the Agency buildings.

"What's he like?"

"You'll find out shortly." Cashel looked at Brio over his glasses. "This is an initial meeting. Brio, not a done deal. He's not cleared for your kind of contract, he's still in training, and you both need to okay all the clauses should you decide to proceed."

"He doesn't want the contract, does he?" Brio could feel himself edging towards hyper.

"He wants what you should want, a compatible arrangement."

"Fuck, Cash, I liked you way more when we were trading blow job disaster stories in that karaoke bar in Memphis."

"We swore never to speak of that night," said Cashel primly.

Brio grinned and settled, turning his face towards the lake. The breeze blew through his hair, cooling the slight sweat on his brow. "He's the closest I've ever seen to being compatible with me. Ash let me run the checks; his sexual pathology is beautiful. His brain has a glow about it, like a nebula," he added wistfully.

Cash tapped him on the arm and nodded his head towards the Agency building. "Your potential Venditor is about to arrive, exactly on time," he said.

Brio turned. An exceptionally tall man in light jeans, plain t-shirt and a casual, forest green jacket, strode towards them. He had a loping gait, his long legs covered the ground quickly, and the sun picked out highlights of gold and bronze in his dirty blond hair.

"That is not a fucking Dom," Brio said. "He's wearing Gucci, for God's sake!"

"Clothing judgment from a millionaire wearing a t-shirt that says. 'I must not stab people with pencils'?"

Brio grinned unrepentantly at Cash.

"Not disappointed, I take it," said Cash mildly.

"Tall is good for a start," said Brio trying to feign nonchalance.

Cash stood and held out his hand as the tall man approached. Brio could see his face was tanned, he had a light scruff on his cheeks, darker than his hair. His smile was easy and open when he grasped Cash's hand. Brio suddenly felt an overwhelming sense of shyness and wished he had worn something less hysterical.

Cashel smiled. "Painter, nice to see you again. This is Brio."

Brio looked up into blue eyes - sky blue, sea blue, glass scoured by the waves under an endless summer day blue. There was green in there too, dark splinters and light splashes, like the prisms of jade in deep water, where the turtles played. Brio found himself rising to his feet without conscious volition.

"Hi." Painter's tone was friendly, but Brio could sense a distance, a misdirection; it made him unhappy. He looked at the hand that Painter held out to him, large, clean nails, long fingers. He would feel those inside him; they would press into him, twist, scissor him open and hold him there. Brio shook his head, trying to force the images away.

He could smell deep, heady notes of cinnamon and amber, dangerously enticing.

Painter was touching him now; his hand grasped Brio's, and his other hand was on his elbow. "I got you." The voice was different now, genuine, and Brio responded to it.

"I'm so sorry. Little bit of a moment there; I think I stood up too quickly, and I didn't have breakfast."

Cashel laughed and covered for him. "I know you were nervous about today."

Painter dropped his hand and stepped back. "Nothing to be nervous about," he said easily, and that distance was back, like a subtle disharmonic. "We're just talking today, nothing to be stressed about."

Brio sat back down. He felt confused, unsure, this guy was giving him mixed signals and not doing anything other than standing there.

"Shall we just jump straight into it?" Cash suggested and indicated Painter should take a seat opposite Brio.

"How are your classes going?" Cashel asked Painter.

"Good, I think," Painter replied. "It's been tough, I won't deny it, it's a lot to take in, but Delphic has great resources; they have people giving me a grounding in lots of things."

Cashel smiled encouragingly.

"I had no idea that the Agency had access to all this." Painter shook his head. "Did you know there's a whole wing of training rooms and playrooms?"

"Well, yes, "Cashel laughed, "I spend a lot of time in them."

"Lucky bitch," Brio muttered to himself.

"So, anyway, I'm pleased that it's going well and that you're comfortable to enter contract negotiations with Brio."

Painter laughed. "I don't think I'm ready to take him on just yet." He threw an admiring grin at Brio, who smirked with pride. "But I think I can offer something to the situation at this stage."

"I don't need a full-time dom at this point anyway," Brio said confidently. "I'm good; I'm working well. That thing a few weeks ago was just a blip; I'm fine. Ash was over-reacting as usual!" It wasn't true, but he sensed a reluctance in Painter that put him on edge.

"Why don't we hear from Painter what he thinks he can offer first," Cashel's voice held a mild rebuke, "before you start maintaining you are 'fine.'" Brio hated it when Cash did the air quote thing.

Painter ran a hand through his hair. "Well, I think, looking at the file, that maintenance spankings seemed to have been effective in the past." His expression was open and honest. "I would feel comfortable setting up a schedule to deliver those."

So honored!

Cashel was making notes. "When are you returning home, Brio?" he asked.

"I'm moving out of Ash and Richard's place tomorrow, and that's not soon enough. I can't stand living with a couple who put cock cages through the dishwasher; it's just wrong."

Painter snorted with laughter, and Brio felt a gleeful frisson at making him laugh. Painter smiled flirtatiously at Brio from under his eyelashes; the man was certainly good-looking.

"I think a schedule of maintenance spankings would be a great place to start, so shall we say Painter will start to deliver those every evening starting next Monday?" Cashel was all business.

"Yeah." Brio couldn't take his eyes away from Painter. Painter's expression was openly admiring now. Brio blushed under his hot stare.

"Does that work for you, Painter?"

"Sorry, what?"

"Are you happy to start delivering maintenance spankings to Brio from next Monday evening?" Cashel repeated.

Painter seemed to pull himself together. "Yes, yeah, that's good."

"What else are you comfortable with Painter?" Cashel asked.

Painter looked down at his hands, his brow furrowed; Brio wanted to wipe the lines away.

"Right now, I'm taking classes fast, and I'm enjoying them but, and I want to stress this, and I want Brio to hear it, too. No matter what the psych report says, there is a big difference between inclination and competence.

"I want to give this contract what it needs," he glanced at Brio, almost guilty, "but I don't want to be distracted by my own urges, so, at least in the short term, I think I need the contract to be non-sexual on my side."

Cashel raised his eyebrows. "That's commendable, Painter."

Brio couldn't help himself. "Yeah, that's excellent. It's great for me because I just hate it when someone so reluctant gets off on me!"

"I'm not reluctant," Painter looked down at his hands, "I'm just cautious."

"And I'm a sub; I kinda need my Dom to want me!"

"Oh, I want you." Painter turned to him, and just for a moment, Brio saw the creature hiding inside. It thrilled him. "I wanted you the second I saw you. Right now, I want to shut up that smart mouth of yours with my cock and choke you with it." Painter mastered himself with visible effort.

"Do it," breathed Brio and leaned into Painter's space. "Let's see what you've got, Venditor."

Painter's hand was in his hair in microseconds, his fist twisted in the thick dark strands. Brio went with it, going pliant, his head tilting where Painter guided it, his breath coming in gasps.

"Enough." Cashel's voice was like a whipcrack.

"Fuck." Painter released Brio's hair and stood up. "I knew this was a bad idea. It's too soon; I haven't got full control of this yet."

"Sit down." Cashel's voice was back to its usual, mild tone. "Painter is right; it is too soon for him to be considering sexual gratification from this. He is a high-level dominant who is just learning, and you," he leveled a reproachful stare at Brio, "are a little shit with the ability to press buttons. Please stop it!"

"Sorry." Brio wasn't sorry; he knew tonight would be full of fantasies about the big man with the demon inside, that voice, that look, that hand in his hair.

"I think we have covered enough for this session," Cashel said, "And I see Richard is here to pick you up." Brio looked up and saw Richard making his way across the lawn towards them. "I think we can agree that the maintenance spankings are a go. Other activities will come online as and when required for Brio's wellbeing, but Painter will not seek sexual gratification for now."

Painter nodded, silent.

"We'll get there, guys," said Cashel. "You're both complicated, but if we proceed with caution, I think you could have a lovely dynamic."

By the look on his face Painter was far from confident about that, Brio thought.

"Hey," Richard greeted them with an easy smile. "You guys done here?"

"Yes, we were just wrapping up," said Cashel. "How are you?"

"Good. Nice to see you again, Painter." He nudged the seated man with his hip. "Sorry I didn't say goodbye properly last time; I was kind of out of it."

There was a story there that Brio wanted to hear.

Painter was struggling to make eye contact with Richard. "No worries, man. And thanks for the demo; it was really, uh, useful."

"Good," Richard said.

"Hey, how did your doctorate defense go?" Painter asked, clearly trying to return the conversation to normality.

Richard's smile was wide and proud. "It went well. I'm Dr. Gannon now."

"Fantastic, well done." Painter's face lit up with a smile.

"Yeah, a single doctorate," said Brio with more jealousy than he thought he possessed. "I call that a good start."

Painter turned stern blue eyes on Brio. "That was rude. Apologize."

Brio thrilled at the wave of dominance Painter broadcast at him, "Sorry, Richard," he said guiltily. "That was ridiculous of me; I'm in a weird bitch mood."

"Good boy." Painter's voice was lower, softer, and just for Brio. He felt the praise curl around him like a hug.

"I think I'm going to like you," Richard said to Painter.

Brio was in the gym when Painter let himself into the house. His phone, placed strategically within view, flashed a notification when Painter opened the front door by keying in the security code.

Being in the gym was a deliberate move on Brio's part; he didn't want to look as though he had been sitting around waiting for a spanking, and apart from that, exercise helped keep his mind calm. Of course, he was also aware that he looked good in sweatpants and a cut-off t-shirt with his muscles warmed from working over the punchbag. Brio was the first to admit he could be shallow.

Despite the interval when Painter had been training, Brio hadn't lied about feeling okay. He'd been stable, working well with Ash on a new configuration of the primary algorithm. He'd also been doing some private experimentation on the structure of the pre-frontal cortex related to the inhibition of sexual desire. It was a fascinating line of inquiry, and he'd spent the afternoon at the university lab happily poring over brain slices.

Brio was immediately aware when Painter entered the room, and he allowed himself to show off a little as he circled the punch bag on quick feet, his jabs and ducks fluid and graceful. He knew he didn't look like the stereotypical gay sub; he had muscle on his long frame and he was fast and strong. It felt good to know Painter's eyes were on him.

Painter didn't interrupt; he just got in Bio's line of sight and waited to be acknowledged. Brio's heart rate had risen by the time he deigned to stop, and he flicked his sweaty hair out of his eyes before he turned to Painter. The smirk on Painter's face as he leaned against the gym wall made Brio hotter.

"I hope you intend to shower before I get up close and personal."

"Didn't think you cared," Brio bitched.

"Slapping cold sweat, not so appealing." Painter shrugged, and Brio couldn't help smiling.

"It does sound gross when you put it like that." He began to unwrap his hands, pulling at the tape with his teeth to get it started.

"Hey, let me." Painter stepped into his space, and Brio was struck again by his height. Brio edged six-foot, and Painter looked down on him easily.

"You have an awesome set up here," Painter commented, his hands deftly working the tape loose from Brio's fists. "The whole house is amazing; it took me ten minutes to find you. I had to follow the sound of punching and grunts; I thought you'd started without me."

His smile was so easy and charming that Brio felt like a dick for not meeting him at the door. "Sorry. I should have come upstairs; I knew you were here. It was a shitty way to welcome you."

"Not a problem, and it's not a punishable offense, this time." Painter was different this time, more confident and teasing, more settled. His training must be helping him.

"Still, it can't be easy just walking into someone's home like this."

"I've been doing it for ten years." Painter shrugged. "I'm used to finding my way around strange but beautiful houses." He rolled the tape from Brio's hands into a ball. "Still, I wouldn't mind a tour now I have your attention, or would you prefer we get straight down to it, host's choice, just for tonight."

Brio suppressed a shiver. Painter was a lot more upfront than he had expected. He thought there would be a lot more toing and froing before they got into it.

"I think I'm just going to take a quick shower. You can have a look around on your own; it's all open to you."

"Okay." Painter was equable and unphased. "And you've eaten, right?"

"Yeah, I had a meal when I came in from work. I was just going to work out, do, um, the thing with you, and then go to bed."

"Fine, works for me." Painter had his hands in the pockets of his jeans; they might as well have been discussing a lift share. "I'll meet you in the living room – I assume that's the place with the sofas and the fuck off fireplace – when you've had a shower. Wear something light; another pair of sweatpants and a t-shirt should be fine."

Painter's attitude was throwing Brio; it was too calm, too easy, too settled. It was like he was reading from the Spanking 101 textbook but had forgotten or was unwilling to turn on the emotional component. This would be a fucking disaster.

When Brio walked into the living room, Painter stood in front of the fireplace. He had his hands behind his back and was staring into space. When he turned to look at Brio, all trace of the easy-going, lazily charming man of earlier was gone. His gaze was direct and his posture tighter, as if aware of every muscle group in his body, and he'd mastered them all.

"I'll have you over the arm of the sofa." His voice was slower, lower, and Brio was moving before he became aware of it.

"Here?" He indicated the wide cushioned arm of the leather sofa to the left of the fireplace.

"Yes. Bend over it, cross your hands behind your back, feet together."

It had been years since he'd submitted himself to a spanking outside of a club or a hookup.

You never forget your posture though, he thought as he folded himself over the arm of the sofa and settled into position, his left hand holding his right wrist in the small of his back.

"Good boy." Painter was closer. Brio shivered at the praise, so longed for, so missed.

He closed his eyes and tried to banish the excitement; this was just a maintenance spanking, nothing to get excited about, just something to settle him, something to get used to again.

"What's your safeword, Brio?"

"Cabbage."

"That has got to be the crappiest safeword on the planet!" There was a hint of Painter's previous humor, and Brio felt a giggle bubbling up.

"My grandmother always said I was not so green as I was cabbage looking."

"She was probably right." Painter's hand rested on Brio's clasped wrists. His skin was warm and dry and the touch comforted. "Are you using your safeword, Brio?"

"No, sir," the honorific was purely instinctual.

"I'm going to pull your pants down and tuck your t-shirt up. I expect you to hold your t-shirt, don't let it go, and don't move your hands from behind your back. Do you understand?"

"Yes, sir." Brio could feel the familiar tension coiling through him, nervous energy in his gut, a buzzing in his ears. He wanted this more than he was prepared to admit.

"I'm going to warm you up with three strikes to either side and then we'll take it from there."

"How many are you giving me, sir?"

"As many as I need to get the result I want."

If Brio didn't know better, he would think that Painter had done this every day for the last decade. His voice didn't display a quiver of doubt. His energy was alluring; it spread out and hauled Brio in, making him feel cared for before a single stroke landed.

He jerked and gasped when his pants were eased down. Painter's hand on his wrists quietened him. "Still, Brio, I want you to keep still for me. Can you do that?"

"Yes."

"I didn't hear you, Brio." There was a threat in the voice now, a promise of disappointment. Brio didn't want that.

"Yes, sir."

"Good boy." Brio breathed again. "Now hold your t-shirt for me." Brio felt the hem of his t-shirt lift, and he grasped the edge of it firmly with his right hand.

"I'm going to begin now."

The first stroke to his left ass cheek stung and was gone, the pain a soothing surge of sunshine on a cold day, just enough to warm. The next was lower, the same side, on his sit spot, and Brio arched luxuriously into it. *So good.* The sound of the hand on his flesh was like music waking him up.

The third smack on the left side was deliciously warm and left a lingering heat.

Painter moved on to strike three times on the right side before he stroked the curves of Brio's ass soothingly. "That was great, Brio. You've got a little bit of color now, so we're going to go harder." Brio shivered. "I don't want you to be quiet, I want to hear you, but I do need you to keep still for me."

"Yes, sir."

Brio knew better than to brace himself. If you tightened the muscles, it hurt more. But he was out of practice and tensed just before Painter landed the first solid spank. It was a corker.

Brio gasped, going up on his toes, surprised by the force.

"Settle, Brio." Painter's voice was heavy and impossible to disobey, and his hand landed on Brio's wrists, holding him down.

"Color?"

"Green," Brio gasped. "God, green."

The next blow landed. Brio cried out. *So good, so bad, such heat.* Painter's hands were big, they covered a wide area, and he wasn't holding back, but he didn't concentrate on just one spot. He worked Brio over evenly, thoroughly. Whoever had taught him was a fucking expert.

Within minutes the pain was a flickering living thing wrapping around Brio. His ass smarted, his breath came in gasps, and his eyes welled with tears, but he clenched his jaw and held his position.

"Good boy, you're doing so well, taking it so well." Painter's voice was thick, his tone deeper than ever. His pleasure in Brio was so apparent it filled Brio's dried-up little heart, and he wanted to weep for the good boy he could be.

He sobbed at the next stroke, dropping his head and raising his hips, lifting himself towards the pain. It had been so long since he'd felt this.

Brio was tired and worn out from fighting himself. The pain was a living thing that teased and burned him and built and built with every stroke. Then the pain was gone, and he was crying, gulping out great heaving sobs; the heat wrapped around him, cocooning him.

Then there were praises being whispered, and Brio realized he was being held, stroked, and told how good he was. Painter had slid onto the sofa and pulled Brio into his arms, nestled him against his chest. He was massaging his hands which felt tight and cramped from holding on to the back of his t-shirt.

The rest of the scene was fuzzy. Brio remembered Painter encouraging him to his feet and supported him through to his bedroom.

Painter wiped his face, then undressed him, and Brio remembered that his cock had been hard; it'd been hard from the first stroke of Painter's hand on his ass. Painter resolutely ignored Brio's erection as he tucked him between the cool sheets. He'd been sad about that. He didn't want Painter to ignore his arousal. Brio would have welcomed Painter doing something with it, just for himself. He thought he suggested as much, but Painter told him to go to sleep.

"I will stay here to make sure you are okay," Painter said before pressed a chaste kiss to Brio's forehead. "Sleep now, little genius, you need your rest." Brio rolled over, curled up, and slept.

Chapter Four

Painter and the reliable erection

Brio's breaths were steady and even, and he slept deeply, curled into a question mark on the bed. Painter could see the elegant line of his long limbs through the thin sheets.

Painter's hand stung, the palm burned despite the conditioning he'd given it lately. It didn't burn as hard or as hot as his arousal, and he hated himself for it.

Brio had been perfect. Well, Brio had been perfectly Brio. Painter liked that. The mercurial mood changes, the snark, and the insecurity tempered his frightening intellect and physical beauty.

He had been all front in the gym, putting on a show and demonstrating that Painter did not have the upper hand. But in the living room, when he'd folded himself over the arm of the sofa and bent his arms behind his back, the act dropped away. The man had called to Painter without opening his mouth.

Painter rose quietly from his watch over Brio and moved out of the room. He needed to explore the house and get the lay of the land because it appeared he would be spending a lot of time here.

Painter had resided in plenty of opulent homes – and opulent yachts and opulent cabins and on one memorable contract, an opulent plane. He was used to the tastes of the rich and bland who bought someone else's vision for their homes. Brio's home was different. The house itself was cutting-edge modern, glass and chrome with views of the city below and the snow-capped mountains in the distance, but it was also uniquely Brio. The kitchen was packed with gadgets – Painter blew a mental kiss to the state-of-the-art coffee machine. It was tempered by a shelf full of tattered cookery books covering every cuisine from classical French to modern Turkish, and the collection of clockwork egg timers lined up on the beam over the range.

Painter picked one up, a yolk yellow plastic pot with an orange chicken on the top. The timer clicked over to zero, and the pot vibrated wildly in his hand as the plastic chicken beg squawked loudly.

"Shit." Painter clamped his hand over the offensively loud thing and rotated the top until he managed to turn it off. He smiled as he carefully put it back in place.

Off the kitchen was a pantry with shelves packed with actual ingredients and staples. *Fuck,* Brio even had linseeds and flax seeds; Painter felt a batch of his signature home-made granola coming on.

He wandered out into the huge living room and tried to ignore the leather sofa where he had bent Brio over. God, the man had been so sensual, even in sweatpants and a simple t-shirt. The graceful way his arms had settled into the bow of his lower back, the enticing curve of his buttocks Painter revealed when he eased his pants down. Plump and round, fuller than the rest of Brio's slender frame, the twin globes had been pale and luminous in the low light until Painter made them glow with a fiery passion. His cock stirred again, and he reached down to adjust himself.

Becoming aroused from domination was something he was slowly accepting. God knows he had spent most of the last three weeks with a persistent erection as he went through training in BDSM techniques and protocols.

Bearing that in mind, he went in search of the playroom suite that Ash had told him was on the lower level of the house. He had to familiarise himself with the space so he could discuss it with his instructor and consider any changes he felt would be appropriate.

As he made his way down the stairway with its steel and wire handrail, he knew it was now a foregone conclusion that he would take the contract. Training had been tough but enlightening; his instructor, Tay, was awesome. He liked the guy a lot; he was straight with Painter, which helped. He didn't dismiss Painter's concerns and issues out of hand as Ash did. Painter didn't think Ash meant to be dismissive, but the man was comfortable in his skin, sexuality, and his relationship with Richard. He couldn't understand why Painter didn't like his Dominant nature.

Painter felt that Ash secretly thought he was stupid, and that galled him. Okay, he wasn't in the same league as Brio, Ash, and Richard, but he wasn't an idiot. Or at least he hoped he wasn't, although, given the way he'd suppressed his nature so effectively, the jury was still out on his self-perception.

The playroom suite was at the other end of the corridor from the gym. By the side of the unobtrusive door, a glass wall looked out over a night lit reflecting pool, all dark water, and moonlit gravel. The wall was cantilevered so it could be swung open, and the pool reached from this level. It would be a pleasant and tranquil place to sit and relax, either before or after scenes – Tay stressed that Painter needed to develop a calm center and recommended yoga and meditation.

Painter opened the door to the play suite, and lights automatically flickered to life.

He didn't know exactly to expect; he had no frame of reference other than porn which Tay had told him to stop watching immediately. So far, he and Tay had worked in a room that resembled a gym as much as anything.

Tay had said he would be taking him to a local club soon to see real-life situations. Painter imagined that would give him more insight into play spaces, but right now, he had one in front of him and needed to nut up and explore it.

With a mental squaring of his shoulders, he stepping into Brio's play space and looked around.

He knew there was more than one room, so he crossed the playroom to explore the furthest spaces first. Off the main play area, he found a small, cozy bedroom. A four-poster bed without a canopy nearly filled the whole room; it sat below a glass skylight. The floor was thickly carpeted, and the colors were muted gold and grey, calming and intimate.

Next to the bedroom was a genuine playroom. When it all got too much for Brio, the contract said he regressed to a childlike state. The large bank of glass doors out onto the garden would make this a bright room during the day. Across three walls ran a vibrant mural of dinosaurs with a volcano blowing its top. Smoke and lava bombs trailed across the ceiling. There was a bookcase crammed with well-thumbed books and a Jurassic World's worth of dinosaur models battling for control of the earth on a play mat.

There was a low day bed made up with linens emblazoned with a very irritated velociraptor. He picked up a plush, stuffed dinosaur that was squatting on an oversized rocking chair – clearly, Little Brio loved dinosaurs.

Painter sighed wistfully. According to the contract, this was a non-sexual thing for Brio, a safe space. Any time Painter was in here, he would be watching over Brio, protecting him, nurturing him. It wasn't a bad thought.

Painter put the stuffie back on the rocking chair and went in search of the bathroom.

The huge bathroom proved to be accessible from all three rooms. It was tiled in bumpy white ceramics and floored with thick nonslip cushioned flooring. The massive walk-in shower had an enema attachment, and there was also a sunken tub, a seating area, and a multi-drawer cabinet worryingly full of medical supplies from anti-bacterial wipes to disposable suture kits.

Finally, he made his way back to the main play area, ready to give it the attention it deserved.

Within seconds of starting to explore the room, Painter's cock chubbed up in his jeans.

The room was large and windowless; the two longest walls were brick painted a warm off white, the floor was both sprung and padded, and the ceiling was a midnight blue gloss crossed with tracked lighting and sliders that held anchor points of metal rings and hooks.

One wall had a range of modern handleless cabinets and drawers. When Painter pressed the exterior of a drawer, it slid out silently to reveal a carefully sorted collection of plugs, vibrators, and dildos. Other cabinets held ropes – a stunning variety, all soft and well prepared – manacles and gags, spreader bars, and impact toys of every description.

A man-sized cage and a versatile spanking bench upholstered in blue leather completed the big play furniture. One corner of the room was set up as a seating and recovery area. A single leather armchair had a kneeling pillow positioned beside it, and there was a small fridge next to a wide sofa with a plethora of throws, quilts, and pillows.

However, the two shorter walls sent Painter's arousal from simmering to a full-on erection. One was a wall of built-in restraints on slide-out blocks that allowed the dominant to arrange the sub however he wanted, as open and accessible as desired.

Opposite this wall, in front of the blue leather spanking bench, was a dark paneled wall inset with a floor-to-ceiling mirror. A Sub on the bench would see their submission reflected in it, while the Dom could watch themselves take...

Stop anonymizing this, Painter said to himself. Man up and admit it; it will be you and Brio in this room. You will watch yourself dominating him; he will watch himself submitting to you.

Whoever put the mirror there knew how to play with humiliation and power, the two edges of this d/s blade.

It wasn't always the complicated shit that caused the hottest scenarios. That mirror was simply perfect.

If Brio was on his knees sucking him off, Painter could admire his beautiful back and gorgeous ass. He palmed himself through his jeans. Spanking Brio earlier had left him thrumming with arousal. Brio had been beautifully hard when Painter put him to bed, but it had been nothing compared to the erection still trying to bite its way out of Painter's jeans.

He leaned against the spanking bench – it was the perfect cock height for him – and considered the mirror. He imagined Brio on the bench, restrained ass up, his skin slick with hot sweat as Painter worked him over with his hand. Every time Brio raised his head, he would see himself in the mirror. Tied down and vulnerable, his eyes would be dark with arousal and swimming with tears. He would see Painter behind him, see every time he raised his hand, and know the next strike was imminent.

Before he knew it, Painter stood at the foot of the bench with his hard cock in his hand. He looked down at his hand working steadily over his long length. He pressed his cock down and rubbed the wet tip against the grained blue leather of the bench. It left a dark stripe behind.

It was no feat of the imagination to imagine the panting sounds Brio would make when Painter roughly spread his hot cheeks apart and rested his cock on his hole. Brio would look up, his eyes meeting Painter's in the mirror.

Painter imagined the look on Brio's face, his mouth hanging open and his eyes begging for more.

He groaned softly, his hand speeding up. Brio's ass had been so hot under his hand, the abused flesh red and radiating. Painter would drape himself over Brio's back, grind his cock against his pain. He'd reach forward, hook his finger into Brio's mouth, stretch his lips apart. *How do you want it, Brio, ass or mouth?* Not that the answer mattered. Painter would decide, that was all part of the tease.

Tears would track down Brio's face and his obscenely gaping mouth would spill grunts that Painter would pretend to consider.

They would watch each other in the mirror. Painter rutting his cock against Brio, telling him what he would do and how Brio would respond. Brio's eyes would be liquid with submission and he'd arch back against Painter as much as his restraints allowed.

Painter leaned one-handed on the spanking bench now, stripping his cock hard and fast, using only a spit slick palm and pre-come to lubricate the way. He panted, the images of Brio crystal clear in his head.

He would fuck the boy, drive himself into that perfectly positioned pliant body, twist his hand into Brio's shaggy black hair and haul his head back to look him in the eye as Painter took him.

Fuck, fuck, he was going to come. His breaths panted, his lower spine prickled as the tension ratcheting higher between his hip bones. "Yes, oh god, yes." He came all over the blue leather, and in his head, Brio screamed and writhed beneath him all hot skin and tight, convulsing ass.

Tay was running ropes through his hands when Painter entered the training room. He raised a hand in acknowledgment, and a broad smile brightened his usually grim face when he saw Painter had brought coffee. He crossed the room, gratefully taking the venti Painter offered.

"Three espresso shots?" he asked.

"Of course. I like my shibari instructor to be totally wired before he suspends a sub!"

"Fuck off," said Tay without malice. "It would take more than three shots to get me wired, and we don't have to worry anyway. We have the world's most obedient rope bunny today; he could tie himself if I asked."

"But I much prefer it when you do it, sir." A young man had slipped through the door behind Painter. He was small but sturdy, and his smile was sunny and enthusiastic. "But I could do it if you really wanted me to."

"Painter, this is Birch. We're lucky to have him today; he's preparing to go out on one of Cash's specialist contracts." Tay dropped a kiss on the young man's buzz-cut dark hair. "And he is the sweetest sub in the building."

It never ceased to amaze Painter that there was a whole additional dimension to Delphic that he'd never known about despite working for the agency for ten years. Beneath his familiar world of vanilla contracts, regular assessments, and endless bureaucracy, there was another ecosystem of dominants and submissives, specialist contracts, and sexual training.

Tay knocked back his coffee. "Okay, shall we get started little Birch?"

"Yes, sir."

"Okay, strip off, sweetheart, and kneel for me in the center of the mat. I'm going to brief Painter and then we'll join you. Waiting position please, head down."

"Yes, sir."

Tay turned to Painter. "We're going to do a suspension today, not because I think you are ready to do one yet but I want you to see where you are going and how good it can be for the sub."

Painter was once again grateful for Tay structuring their lessons to positively reinforce the dominant aspects of his personality.

If it wasn't for the fantasies, which were impinging on his day-to-day life more and more, Painter would be feeling a lot better about accepting this part of his personality because of Tay.

Tay wiped the remnants of coffee from the corner of his mouth and his voiced lowered. "There is going to be a sexual component to this. it won't involve you in a hands-on way, you'll just be watching, but Cash has instructed that he wants Birch to experience orgasm with two dominants in the room." He glanced over at the boy who now knelt naked on the mat, his posture perfectly relaxed, his hands curled palm up on his spread thighs. "It's something to do with his upcoming specialist contract. I'm going to suspend him, edge him a little bit, nothing too intense, and then let him orgasm. When he comes, I want you close so he can feel the dynamic, but you don't need to do anything to him.

"I'd also like your help with aftercare; help me rub him down and get him back into his outdoor headspace. He's a placid little thing, real even-tempered, so he won't be hard work. He bounces back real quick from stuff like this and trots off happy as a lamb usually."

"You say usually, could two doms be a problem?"

Tay smiled, obviously pleased that Painter had spotted the possible pitfall. "I don't think it will be a problem. He knows me well and trusts me. He knows I won't share him with you nor get anything out of this myself."

"What if he safewords?"

Tay picks up on Painter's unspoken question. "If either of you safeword the usual protocols apply, everything stops, Birch gets cut out of the ropes, and everyone regroups and talks about it."

"Got it."

"Okay, we're going to start. I'll talk you through the ties and the anchors; Birch will go all dopey in the rope but if you have questions, please respect his headspace and be sensitive, I know you will, but it bears mentioning."

Painter gave Tay a more confident thumbs up than he felt.

As Tay said, Birch was, without questions, an utter rope bunny. Before Tay had finished weaving the harness around his chest, Birch was doe-eyed and dopey. He moved fluidly under Tay's whispered instructions, and by the time Tay encouraged him to his feet and tied the first suspension line from the chest tie to the ceiling ring, Birch was deep in subspace.

A second line to his left foot had Birch up on the toes of his right and pirouetting lazily in space. The boy's cock steadily engorged as Tay wrapped more rope around him.

Tay repeatedly checked the tension and placement of knots, letting one rope take the strain to allow him to move another, adjusting Birch's position until the boy floated just how he wanted him. Painter shadowed Tay, taking in the techniques, the energy, the give and take between Dom and Sub.

Eventually, Birch was fully suspended, his body an elegant curve rotating in the air.

Tay set the boy twirling gently on his ropes with a light push and beckoned Painter over.

"Gorgeous, isn't he?" Tay said quietly in Painter's ear.

Painter had to agree. The bindings highlighted Birch's solid musculature. The chest harness showed off the breadth of his shoulders, and the narrowness of his waist and the ankle rope and thigh line caused his legs to spread and flex, directing attention towards his groin.

The boy's cock, plump and pretty, was fully erect against his stomach, and his round, tight balls were vulnerable and exposed by the suspension position.

Painter swallowed, imagining Brio like this. He could have Brio like this if he wanted.

Would Brio be quiet and submissive within the hold of the rope, or would he be challenging and fearless?

He imagined Brio's rich mop of hair instead of Birch's close crop. He'd grab hold of it, move Brio within the air, holding his head at just the right angle so he could fuck into that wise-ass mouth.

"Painter, you with me?"

"Yeah, yeah, sorry." Painter dragged his attention back to his instructor.

Tay's huge hand was on his arm. "It's okay, I get it, it's distracting as all hell, but you have to keep focus. I'm going to edge him now, and I want you right beside me."

Together Tay and Painter moved towards the suspended sub. Tay laying a hand on his flank and turning him towards them. "Hey, baby boy," he crooned. "Feel good?"

"Mmmm." Birch's head hung back and he struggled to open his eyes, but smiled sweetly at Tay. "Yeah, Tay, feels awesome."

"You look beautiful, Birch," Painter added, stepping in so Birch knew he was there. "Just gorgeous."

"Wanna fuck me?" Birch's eyes were dark, his lips red with arousal.

"Not today, sweetheart," Painter said.

"This is just for you today," Tay added and bent down to press a kiss to the sub's forehead. "This is just to make you feel extra nice because you've been so good."

"Thank you." Birch's voice slurred and he arched lazily in his bonds, swirling slowly.

Tay moved away to get lube before positioning himself between Birch's thighs. He bent and blew gently on the boy's balls before taking hold of his cock with a lube slicked hand and slowly pumping his erection.

Birch moaned soft and low, and his head fell back again.

Tay teased Birch gently, praising him and slowly bringing him closer and closer to orgasm. It wasn't an intense session where Birch would have been brought to the peak and then denied again and again.

Instead, Tay worked Birch through a slow, incessant rise, a gradual climbing until Birch was held right on the edge, slowly gasping.

Tay motioned for Painter to go to Birch's head. He cupped his hands around Birch's smooth skull and lifted the boy's head. "You ready to come, Birch?" he asked, and glanced at Tay who nodded his approval. "You want Tay to make you come now?"

"Oh, yes, please," Birch's voice was a breathy whisper.

"Okay, Birch, come when you like, sweetheart."

Painter glanced down Birch's body to see Tay's hand speeding up. When he turned back to Birch, the boy locked eyes with him. Painter could feel the tension in the boy's neck, the urgent vibration in his body. Birch held his breath, his body bowed, and with a soft cry, he came.

"Good boy," Painter praised him and stroked his face, wishing he held Brio instead.

As Tay had said, Birch was a resilient little sub; once lowered and out of the ropes, he bounced back quickly, needing only minimal aftercare. Painter took care of the ropes while Birch, back in his sweats, snuggled with Tay on the recovery mat and cheerfully gobbled down squares of chocolate.

Eventually, Tay got up and stretched. "You did well, kiddo," he said to Birch. "You were really good."

"I'm always good." Birch grinned cheekily as he picked up his bag and headed out of the training room.

Tay shook his head and turned to Painter. "How was that for you?"

"It was good, I found it useful, and Birch was really good."

"Yeah, as he says, he's always good." Tay looked at Painter calculatingly. "It's a shame really; I'd like him to be naughtier so I could hurt him more."

Painter said nothing, just stared evenly at Tay until the man quirked a smile and turned away, obviously having seen all he needed.

Painter spent the remainder of the day thinking about Tay's comment. It resonated with him. He had felt that desire to hurt, to inflict pain, in himself more and more lately.

At night, in his dreams, he fucked Brio. When he reached around to cup him while buried to the root in his ass, Brio's cock was soft, small, and vulnerable, and Painter loved it.

He hated that dream.

Chapter Five

Brio and the need for knots

"I went for lunch with Richard today," Brio said. "Honestly, if he gets any more serious, FEMA will be camped around him waiting for an emergency to be declared."

"Leave him alone," said Painter. "He is the most normal person I've met in the last six weeks." He paused, a blush staining his cheeks. "Apart from the first ten minutes after I met him, those weren't normal at all."

Brio giggled. "I heard."

"So much for confidentiality at Delphic. The sub support system has been gossiping again."

Brio nibbled at the sandwiches he'd made for Painter and himself. He had spent an hour constructing them because the day, even with a lunch date with Richard, had been vile.

Thinking of Richard reminded him that Ash's husband had been very straight with his opinions on Painter. Brio hadn't wanted Richard's opinions; his contract with Painter was so tenuous that he hadn't dared push on anything despite the need growing in him.

"How was he anyway?" Painter asked.

"Opinionated."

"I hear friends can be like that," Painter said mildly.

"I told him to fuck off."

Painter gave Brio a disapproving look. "That must have upset him."

"Hard to tell with Richard." Brio nibbled more of his sandwich and fidgeted in his seat. "Some people have resting bitch face, Richard has a resting professor of theology listening to a student deliver a paper on the religious symbolism in medieval literature that he bought off a Philippino guy on Fiverr, face."

Painter's brow wrinkled as he parsed his way through the sentence. "Unless Ash is in the room," he said.

"Yes, unless Ash in the room and then it's like someone mainlined him full of smiles, it's ridiculous."

"That's love for you."

"Boy, you're Mr. Cognizant tonight."

"I have no idea what that means," Painter said placidly. "But I do know you are cranky. Bad day?"

Brio took a mouthful of his sandwich; it was like trying to chew through a pillow. "Yes," he said moodily." Long day, bad day, nothing worked, hypotheses died, my lab tech smelled of Lebanese food, Ash is away, Richard wanted to talk about feelings, general shit day."

Painter continued to chew slowly and watched Brio across the island unit. His expression gave nothing away, but he never took his eyes off Brio.

"Do you think submissives are weak?" Brio asked.

"No! Brio, no, fuck, I've seen in training just how tough they are." Painter paused, then added with a sheepish smile, "I've seen you in the gym. You didn't look weak to me; you looked hot. Fit. and fast."

"Are you flirting with me, Painter?" Brio gave him his best shit-eating grin.

"Do I need to?" Painter replied equably.

Brio stood up from his seat and rounded the island towards Painter. "Not really," he said with a shrug. "I am notoriously easy."

Painter carried on eating his sandwich, licking mayonnaise off his fingers in a way that drove Brio mad.

Brio leaned casually against the island close to Painter. "Seriously, if I asked you to tie me down, would that make me weak?"

Painter leveled a serious gaze at Brio; his eyes were denim blue in the evening light. "No," he said thickly.

"If I asked you to distract me for a while, so I didn't have to think. Would that make me weak?"

"No. Brio-"

Brio interrupted, his voice low, smoky, and seductive. "If I were to invite you to scene with me tonight, Painter, what would you think?"

Painter licked his lower lip.

Brio could feel the energy between them ramping up. "If I invited you to scene with me, and you rendered me helpless," Brio crooned, "How would that feel to you, Painter?"

"Good," Painter breathed.

"And how much do you think I'd like it?" Brio purred, edging into Painter's space, desperate to touch.

"I think you'd like it very much." Painter placed his sandwich back on the plate and rotated on the stool. His hands settled carefully on Brio's hips; the thumbs pressed lightly on his hip bones. "I think I could make it good for you."

"Would it feel good for you too?"

"What are you..." Painter's look was questioning. "Yes, it would make me feel good."

"Why would it make you feel good?" Brio stroked a finger along Painter's lower lip. "You can be honest with me; it's part of the deal."

Painter's expression was wary. "You know the answer to that is complicated, Brio." His thumbs continued to press on Brio's hips. "And it can change from day to day but right now, making you feel good would make me feel good because you being relaxed and content would make me feel the same way."

"So if I asked for it, if we both got something out of it, would it wrong?"

"Of course not. Not at all."

"Then why do you resist it? Why do you choose not to give me what makes me feel right?" Brio let the sadness and rejection seep into his tone.

There had been nothing sexual yet between them, just the daily maintenance spankings and a growing sexual tension that was now so thick and syrupy you could dish it up with a spoon. Brio wanted more, needed more, but he walked a tightrope of his creation – he could only ask for what Painter would give willingly.

Painter might be a Venditor, but Brio was self-aware enough to know that if he pushed Painter to do something sexual that he wasn't ready for, the fallout for them both would be dire.

Painter's head tilted to one side as he appraised Brio carefully. Brio could see the rapid beating of the pulse in his throat, but the hands on his hips rested casually, and the thumbs stroked soothingly. Brio felt naked under Painter's gaze.

"I would like to scene with you tonight, Brio." Painter's voice was deeper than usual, his phrasing formal. "I would like to restrain you tonight; I would like to tie you. Do you want that?"

"Yes," Brio breathed, his heart rate picking up. "I want that."

"Go to the playroom, get undressed, stand in the center of the room, arms behind your back and your feet shoulder-width apart." Painter's voice was like Kahlua over ice-cream, rich and dark, a good way to melt vanilla. "Will you do that for me?"

"Yes."

Painter quirked an eyebrow at Brio.

"Yes, sir," he said hurriedly.

"Go. I'll be there in five minutes."

Brio went, his insides hot with arousal and nervous anticipation, the rotten day forgotten.

Painter didn't need to know that Brio had never played in this room before. When he stood naked in the center, under the soft glow of the track lighting, it was for the very first time.

The playroom suite had been installed when Brio bought the house, but he had never played there. The only room he went into regularly was the Little Room, and that was only when he had, to when things all got too much.

He had designed this suite, had put all his desires, kinks, and hopes for a future that had never happened into it, but until this evening, it had stood idle. He took a deep breath, hoping that the room would work for them both.

When Painter entered the room Brio maintained his position, his eyes downcast, his posture straight but relaxed. Painter walked over and circled him, Brio could see his bare feet and the bottom of his jeans brushed the padded flooring. Painter had nice feet; the nails were trimmed and the skin was soft, and he had none of those horrible long hairs some people have on their toes. Painter tried, Painter groomed himself, made an effort for his Emptores, even though he was the confessed laziest Venditor at Delphic. Brio thought that was probably untrue.

"Thank you, Brio," Painter's voice was soft, "that position is perfect you did well."

Brio smiled at the floor, gentle heat building inside his chest.

"I'm going to tie you tonight, Brio. It will mean I am touching you is that okay?"

"Yes, sir," Brio breathed.

"I think you will look lovely in a design I have planned." Painter had obviously acquainted himself with the room because he went unerringly to the rope locker.

"You can look up, Brio," he said when he returned. "I want you to see what I am doing, but I would prefer if you didn't speak unless it is important or you need to safeword."

Brio lifted his head. Painter was bare-chested, wearing only his low slung jeans. His chest was well defined without being bulky, his nipple dark tight nubs on his hairless chest. A thin dark line of hair led down from the deep pit of his navel to the waistband of his jeans.

Two coils of rope were slung over his shoulder, and he was running long lengths of gold ribbon through his fingers, all liquid and mesmerizing where the light caught them.

"They gave me these in class, so I could start my design without drowning in rope, and I found I liked it." Painter's voice was almost shy when he added, "I brought it here because I thought it would suit you; I want to see you in ribbon and rope," He bit his lip as if holding in more revelations. Brio stayed silent, just watched the gleaming lengths of gold run through Painter's fingers.

"What's your safeword, Brio?" Painter asked.

"Cabbage, sir."

Painter smiled. "I'm never going to get used to that." He gave a wry shake of his head and stepped forward.

Painter ran his hands all over Brio's naked body as familiarising himself with all the new flesh on display. His warm fingers trailed down Brio's arms, across his belly, then swept down the back of his thighs. The ribbons slipping over Brio's skin caused his cock to swell with interest against his thigh.

Painter wrapped lengths of ribbon around Brio's muscles and tied them in neat bows. The loops curled around the bulge of his biceps, the swell of his calves and thighs. The long tails of the ribbons swayed in the breeze from the ceiling fan, tickling his skin.

Painter circled him like a predator, his steps light on the padded floor, his hands sure when they touched him.

The whole time Painter kept up a steady murmur of instruction and statement, detailing – almost to himself – what he was doing and what would happen next. He stroked the different muscle groups as he went.

It sent Brio to a nice, floaty place, and he was calm and breathing deeply when Painter switched to the ropes. Painter started his tie just below Brio's pectoral muscles. The tails crossed over his spine before they ran up and over his shoulders. The way he moved, slow and methodical but with increasing confidence, played into Brio's desire to be owned.

It was beautiful to watch. His Dom was a natural at the process, becoming consumed by it as he built a neat pattern around Brio's chest and shoulders. The harness was snug, thick and sturdy between his shoulder blades. His arms are free, and he still had nearly his full range of movement. The way Painter looked at him when he was done put logistical thoughts out of Brio's mind.

"Last bit." Painter breathed out heavily and went down on his knees before Brio.

Painter passed the rope around Brio's waist before drawing it up between his legs. The double length of the rope split and ran up either side of his penis and scrotum, applying delightful squeezing pressure to the whole area.

Brio sighed with delight as he felt Painter's hands on his genitals, warm and sure, the new rope calluses dragging on his delicate skin.

His eyes were heavy-lidded as he looked down and watched Painter build an intricate ladder of flat knots from the root of his penis to his waist. Framed like a piece of art, his cock looked amazing, huge and beautifully presented.

"That's so awesome," Painter said and ran a light finger down the Brio's erect cock and up the ladder of ropes.

Brio breathed through his arousal, sinking deeper into it.

Painter rose and moved behind Brio. Tucking his fingers beneath the bottom line of the waist rope, Painter jerked roughly. Brio's dick jumped, and Painter pulled him around to look in the mirror in the playroom wall. Brio was stunned by what he saw.

The ribbons gleamed in the glow of the spotlights, and the ropes were opaque against his skin. They highlighted every bulge of muscle, and there was a hunger on Painter's face that Brio had never seen before. The man's pupils were blown, huge and intense, and he stared at Brio like he was the last drink of water in the desert.

Brio couldn't believe how hot he looked like this. The chest harness felt amazing, and the crotch tie that brought his cock front and center was a work of art. But more than his feeling, was the knowledge that this was very obviously something Painter enjoyed. But most important of all, the so good thought that sent Brio spiraling higher was that Painter had read him. Brio had wanted this, Painter had known, and had given it to him.

The process of creating the patterns had lulled Brio into a calm mindset. The meticulous detail involved in the knotwork, the touching and the tracing of the linework had turned Brio into art. He felt the languid joy of the objectified, made beautiful by what Painter had done.

"See how beautiful you are," Painter's voice was soft in his ear. "Let's make you more beautiful still."

Painter wrapped his hand in the back of the chest harness and pulled Brio backward, walking him back toward the large leather chair in the corner. His grip was tight but not painful; the ropes distributed the force evenly. The sheer mastery of Painter's ropework made arousal coil hot and tight in the pit of Brio's stomach.

"What's your color, Brio?" Painter asked when he stopped in front of the chair.

"Oh green, this is really, really green." Brio rolled his head back to look up at Painter. "You are so good at this, sir."

"Thank you." Painter smiled. Reaching around, he thumbed Brio's nipple between the ropes of the chest harness.

Brio swallowed a whine.

Painter sat back onto the leather armchair, his legs together and his feet flat on the floor. He dragged Brio down to straddle his lap and pulled him back against his chest. "That's better. Now I can reach more of you."

Brio was impossibly aware of his body; he was helpless on Painter's chest, his legs spread open over Painter's thighs, and his rope-framed erection was the main attraction.

Painter's arm was warm around his waist, and he started to play with Brio's nipples, rolling them gently between his fingers and then tugging at them to test their sensitivity.

Brio whimpered. Painter hummed in approval before pinching them harder. Brio's hips twitched, rutting forward.

"Do you want me to touch your cock, Brio?" Painter asked.

"Please, sir."

"You're being so good." Painter's hand slid lower and tugged at the crotch tie that ran between Brio's buttocks and either side of his scrotum.

"I'll always be good, sir," Brio gasped.

"Now we both know that's not true." Painter cupped his balls, tugging them lightly until Brio squirmed in his lap. "And I don't want you to be because then I couldn't punish you." His hand slid up Brio's cock, and he squeezed the head of it. Brio jerked and pre-come pumped out of the tip of his cock and dribbled down the flange.

"Nice," Painter said before he scooped the dribble up with his finger and raised it to his mouth. "You taste sweet," he added after licking his finger clean. "Have you been eating a lot of fruit?"

"Pineapple," Brio struggled to enunciate. "Pineapple smoothy at lunch."

"Well, it makes you taste delicious." Painter's voice was low and so different from his normal tone. "You should have one every day." He reached down again and rubbed at the frenulum of Brio's cock. The sudden burst of sensation made Brio arch back and yelp in pleasure.

He felt so helpless and small on Painter's lap. Despite the simplicity of the tie and his legs being free, Bio felt controlled, positioned, defenseless against the touches Painter chose to give him.

"Oh more, please more, sir."

Painter's hand settled around his cock in a loose grip and began to pump him slowly. It was too dry, his skin, sensitive from the ropes, magnified every drag. It was perfect.

"So good, so good, please don't stop," Brio was babbling and rutting up into Painter's grasp, "Please, tighter, more, more."

"You're such a toppy little bastard," Painter's chuckle was amused, "But you've been such a good boy tonight," His grip tightened, and he added a twist over the head of Brio's cock on the upstroke.

The glide was smoother now, Brio's precome easing the way, and Painter was a fucking expert. He cupped Brio's balls with one hand, tugging on them lightly, while the other slid up and down his cock with perfect friction, the grip was just tight enough, and his thumb flicked at the sensitive frenulum.

"Oh god, please can I come?" Brio leaned back on Painter's wide chest, and his splayed thighs quivered, the muscles jerking as he tried to rut up into Painter's touch.

"Because you asked, because you didn't just let go, you can come."

Brio was overjoyed. "Oh, thank you, I didn't think you'd let me."

"I won't always." Painter sounded almost amused. "But tonight, I will. Come for me, baby, come now."

The orgasm that hit Brio was like being washed away by a wave. He held his breath as his body jerked and his come shot over his belly and Painter's hand. He could feel the rope between his buttocks rubbing against his spasming asshole, and he let out a long, low groan as Painter worked him through the shockwaves.

"Beautiful, Brio." Painter's croon was a warm blanket wrapping round Brio. "That was gorgeous; I am so pleased with you,"

Brio relaxed back on Painter's chest and tilted his head to look him in the face.

"You were awesome," he whispered, and Painter's smile filled him with as much pleasure as the orgasm.

Painter stroked Brio's hair off his forehead. "We'd better get you out of these ropes and cleaned up. It's nearly time for your spanking."

"Don't need spanking tonight," Brio said lazily. "Totally chilled out and good now thanks."

"What makes you think the spanking is just for you?"

"Not fair," Brio complained. "I've been good; I shouldn't have to be spanked. Please, Painter," He gave Painter his best sweet submissive look.

"You are so beguiling when you do that." Painter pressed a kiss to his forehead. "It makes the thought of reddening your ass even nicer."

"Sadist."

"Apparently so, and after this scene, I'm feeling pretty dom'd up so expect a blistering."

Chapter Six

Painter and the hot flesh beneath his hand

What a night, Painter thought, what an eye-opening, crotch-tightening, flesh-tingling night. His palm still stung from Brio's pre-bedtime spanking, and he could still smell him on his skin.

He was too wired to go home and sleep, too aroused. And God, he loved that arousal; he wanted to keep it glowing inside him by feeding it memories of Brio in the rope to make it flare. Wandered around Brio's house in the semi-dark, he took in the distant lights of the city from the wide windows prowling the rooms like a dominant guard dog patrolling the perimeter of his domain.

He liked it here. He liked the house, he liked Brio, and he really liked what they did together. Spanking Brio wasn't just a turn-on; it was fucking delicious.

And the shibari, bloody hell, who knew just tying someone up made you feel like that? Seeing Brio standing pliant and patient within his ribbons and ropes, willingly putting himself in Painter's hands, had made him feel both powerful and privileged.

He hadn't expected the actual domination to feel like that. In his imagination, he had thought it would be a technical exercise – do this, tie that, be safe, make pretty – but the reality was so much more. Experiencing the give and take of energy between himself and Brio, that entwining connection, could get addictive, real quick.

Painter's instruction at Delphic was proceeding at an astonishing speed, impact play, sensation play, shibari, and consent, but the big thing he realized was that the other subs he interacted with during training didn't hold a candle to Brio. Brio's body was interesting to Painter in ways no one else had ever been. It produced new sensations in his being, awakened feelings and instincts he didn't know he possessed.

Just seeing Brio naked and vulnerable, knowing he was in charge and responsible for working out ways to do what they both desired, not only had him hard in his shorts but made him hazy on why he had been so reluctant to do this.

His life had changed in profound ways, and he didn't think he could go back to the way it had been before. This was his new normal, and he had no idea how he felt about that.

He wandered into the kitchen and leaned on the worktops looking out into the night, his face a ghost against the black glass. He should be tired, but he wasn't. He felt full of energy and couldn't stop the small smile the played across his lips. *Why am I so happy?*

This contract had already run weeks past what he was used to; being more settled in life hadn't proved to be the bad thing he'd imagined. He was staying in one place for the foreseeable future rather than skipping around the globe on short-term contracts. He'd made a new and solid connection with Tay, his trainer. They were going to a club on Thursday because there werw some things Tay just couldn't ethically demonstrate in the training environment. Plus, he thought that Richard, if not Ash, could become a friend if the contract went on much longer.

Friends... the idea felt almost alien to him. When did he last make friends rather than have interactions? *How did I not noticed that I was so damn lonely?*

Painter pushed away from the worktop and paced quietly towards Brio's room, feeling the need to check on the man. *I'm just doing a good job, just being thorough and delivering appropriate aftercare.*

Painter watched Brio from the bedroom door. He didn't know how long he stood there watching Brio breathe steadily in his sleep, sprawled across the sheets, dark head pressed into the pillow and his hands tucked under his chin.

Brio snuffled, his eyes blinked open sleepily, and he smiled at Painter.

"Go back to sleep, baby," Painter said quietly from the doorway. Brio, obedient, passive, not awake, closed his eyes again and snuggled back into his pillow.

Unfamiliar contentment warmed Painter - when he tied Brio, when he touched Brio, when he gave him pleasure then spanked him and put him to bed, it felt more than a job well done.

Reluctantly, Painter turned away from the bedroom, collected his duffle bag, and quietly let himself out of the house. As he climbed into his car, he reminded himself that this was work, weird work, but work nonetheless. Because of it, he had a nice apartment, a nice car, nice clothes, and he didn't have to take a proper job; it was all good. *Why, if it's all good, does leaving Brio alone in his bed feel so bad?*

"Nice digs," Tay said when Painter joined him in front of his apartment building.

"Been a Venditor a long time." Painter shrugged and looked up at the building, "This is the most time I've spent in it since I bought it; normally I'm off doing contracts."

"You only ever did short-term?"

"Yeah, it felt safer." Painter found he could admit things to Tay that he'd been unable to voice before. Maybe it was because Tay was so easy about being a professional Dom; he made it seem okay, layered it with rules and safety protocols.

"Me too," Tay admitted, "I only did short-term before I began training. You okay with walking to the club? It's not that far."

"No problems." The night air was cool and brisk; it always was here, the city was so high. Painter wore a leather jacket over his button-down shirt; the jacket was his only concession to their destination. Tay wore leather trousers, skin tight to his impressive thighs, and spit-shined black knee-length boots. His look was still vanilla enough for a walk through the downtown streets.

They started down the street, an easy camaraderie between them.

"What's the plan for tonight?" Painter asked eventually.

"Well, I think it's important that you see a corporal punishment scene, and that's not something I am comfortable delivering within a training environment as I don't have a sub of my own at the moment."

"Explain, please." Painter had discovered that Tay was good with short, direct questions; it seemed to trigger an automatic flood of information, and Painter just soaked it up.

"Rules are good in the kind of contracts we do, and by extension, D/S relationships in general. Rules make subs feel safe within the boundaries, and doms like building them around their subs. However, a punishment scene for rule-breaking has a very different vibe to pain play.

"Right now, you give Brio daily spankings that are a bridge between pain play and punishment scenes."

"So me spanking Brio every day is a rule?"

"Yeah. It's been created by negotiation; you know about it, he knows about it, it serves a purpose and is delivered calmly without prejudice. Everybody knows where they stand. You will add more rules as you progress in your contract, and those will come with rewards for compliance and punishments for disobedience."

Painter nodded. He could feel the shape of that in his head, how it would work, a weaving of give and take between him and Brio.

"You've seen me do impact play for fun," Tay said. "You've seen me use a light flogger for sensation play, and you've seen my work with subs who like the pain. We've covered all of that, but tonight's dynamic is different; it's punishment, a firm response to rule-breaking."

"What does the sub get out of it?"

Tay glanced at Painter. "Interesting that you don't feel the need to ask what the dom gets out of it."

Painter shrugged. "I'm kinda getting used to the idea that I would get something very significant out of a situation like that."

Tay paused, and Painter stopped too, turning to face his instructor. "The sub gets their transgression wiped away, their guilt removed, and the rules around them reinforced; it makes them feel safe.

"They also get to suffer for their Dom because people like us, we like it, and our subs know that. What stops us from being monsters is that we don't do it randomly. We do it with care and attention and within the context of an established and agreed dynamic." Tay's gaze was serious. "You must understand this Paint, this thing we are and this thing we do, it's called a power exchange for a reason, it's a free choice, and fair exchange is no robbery. You get that, right?"

Painter nodded but knew he didn't quite get it, not the way Tay wanted him to. Tay knew it too, and his expression was rueful. "Look, we're going to go watch a scene. A friend of mine is punishing his sub tonight with a caning because his sub broke the rules they had agreed on. This punishment will be semi-public, with a few people in one of the private rooms because that is what they agreed on. We're witnessing it, and we need to understand how much trust the sub is putting in his dom to agree to that; it's a highly emotional thing, top of the intense tree."

Painter nodded dumbly, his shoulders hunched, his hand deep in his pockets.

"Afterward, we'll talk about it, and you get to tell me how you feel." He grinned. "I think I might be turning into Cashel; I've been spending way too much time with the guy."

The club was exactly as Painter had imagined, from the low lights and cheesy décor to the crowd of semi-dressed patrons and the smell of sexual potential and hot bodies.

Tay signed him in and gave him a quick guided tour – cloakroom, bar area with mingling space, and small stage area for demonstrations. There were public play areas and a corridor of rooms for private scenes and aftercare.

After getting a couple of beers from the bar, Tay guided Painter to a booth at the back of the mingling area. As they moved through the crowd, a few leather-clad men nodded at Tay, and a disconcerting number of subs, obvious by their attire, gave him the side-eye as he passed.

Music played in the background but not loud enough that Painter couldn't hear Tay when they settled into the booth.

"You come here often?" Painter asked.

"Not as much as I used to," Tay said, taking a long swallow of his beer. "I used to play here back in the day, but I'm not playing outside of training at the moment," Painter sensed a story here but didn't push Tay to explain.

"Okay." Tay switched into trainer mode. "What you need to remember about caning is the cane itself decides the stroke. When you choose a cane, you need to think about the result you want, and you need to practice. You don't just pick one up and start whaling on somebody."

Tay went on to give the pros and cons of various canes, where on the body they worked best, and how to use them efficiently and safely. Painter made mental notes, but all the time, his excitement level rose. Over on the stage, a sweet-looking blonde was using a deerskin flogger on her older male sub; the sound of the tails on his skin was waking Painter's dom up. He could see the flinch and tense in the sub's shoulders as he held his position, hands on his head and feet shoulder-width apart. The dom circled him, her step light as though dancing. The flick of the flogger, the sing of it, the kiss of it on reddening flesh mesmerized him. When she started to flog her sub's cock into an erection, Painter had to put his hand against his groin and press down on his semi.

"You ready?" Tay's question made Painter jump, and he licked dry lips, dragging his eyes away from the stage.

"It's different in this environment," said Tay. "It's always more intense in clubs and at home, quite different to the training rooms."

"Yeah," Painter agreed. "Any last-minute instructions?" he asked as he and Tay got to their feet and made their way through the crowd to the back of the club.

"Say nothing, do nothing, watch and learn."

The private room had ten people arranged around the edges, talking quietly in couples or waiting with serious expressions.

In the center of the room, a well-built man was restrained in wooden stocks, bent over, his head and hands clamped in place, and his feet cuffed to a spreader bar. His not unsubstantial cock and balls hung below his well-muscled ass.

His skin shone with sweat under the central light in the room. Painter couldn't see his face; hair covered his features as his head hung down. The sub's hair was thick and tousled, like Brio's, and the dark brother inside Painter's head growled happily.

With a hand on his elbow, Tay guided him to the side of the room, level with the restrained man's waist.

"We're going to move around during the scene," he murmured in Painter's ear. "I want you to get a good view from all angles."

Painter nodded.

When the Dom entered the room, Painter was surprised; he was older, significantly lighter than his sub, middle-aged with silver hair. He held a long cane in one leather-gloved hand and wore dark jeans and boots; his chest was bare. Painter hoped he'd look that good when this guy's age.

The Dom ignored the people in the room and went straight to his restrained sub. He crouched in front of the man, looking up at him, speaking quietly, and brushing hair out of his eyes.

Painter could feel the tension and excitement in the room swell; he fought his desire to sink into the feeling being generated.

When the sub shivered and nodded, Painter realized he was holding his breath. He let it out slowly and rotated his shoulders to ease the tension.

The Dom moved around behind his sub, his hand trailing along the man's flank. He positioned himself behind and to the side of the man, opposite Tay, and Painter.

"Twenty strikes for rule-breaking," he said, his voice even, almost dispassionate. "Agreed?"

"Yes, sir," the sub's voice was quiet, desperate. Painter shivered at the need in it.

"Color?"

"Green, sir."

The silver-haired man placed the cane against the sub's ass, measuring the distance. He drew his arm back, his wrist flexed, and the first strike landed with a hum and a crack.

The sub screamed, jerked in his bonds. Painter was hard as rock instantly, so hard, and his heart hammered. The energy in the room spiked with collective arousal.

Next to him, Tay drew in a breath that was almost a groan.

Afterward, Painter couldn't have said how long it lasted. Tay carefully and quietly moved him around the room. Painter followed in a daze, taking in minute details and soaking in the sinister joy of it all.

He saw how perfectly the dom laid down parallel lines on his sub's lower ass and thighs. He admired the rising red swell of them and let out a hum of admiration when the Dom paused and pressed his fingers into the welts, and the sub cried out at the change in sensation.

The sub's growing screams were heady music to his ears, and his cock was so hard he didn't dare touch himself to adjust it where it pressed against the inside of his jeans.

When the screams stopped, and the Dom went to his knees in front of his sub, praising and comforting the sobbing, crying man, Painter let out a sigh of profound joy. "Beautiful," he breathed, unable to help himself.

With a hand on his back, Tay encouraged him from the room and out of the club. On the sidewalk, Painter leaned back against the club's wall and drew in deep breaths of cool night air. He felt distant, fuzzy, horny as hell, and disgusted with himself. He had just watched a man he didn't know being intimately punished, and his cock was still hard and pulsing in his jeans.

Tay leaned against the wall beside him. "Times like this, I wish I still smoked."

Painter knew what he meant.

"You okay?" Tay asked.

"Yeah, that was fucking intense; way more than I expected."

"Sometimes it's like that. The energy was really high in there."

"It was crazy." The darkness in Painter's head was receding, but the beginning of a headache pulsed at his temples. "I can't see myself doing that."

"Try not to lie to yourself, Painter. It's not helpful at this stage." Tay sounded disappointed in him.

Painter ran a hand through his hair. "Yeah, that was a total lie, wasn't it?"

Tay shrugged. "You're doing well, Paint, but it's late in the day for you to be acknowledging this side of yourself; it's bound to be tough – no pun intended."

Painter managed to grin at that.

"Let's go and get coffee," said Tay. "And we'll talk about rules you can consider setting up with your boy; it's time. A contract like this without rules is chaos at best and abuse at worst."

Painter nodded.

"Tomorrow, we'll go over the safety aspects of what you just saw once it's had a chance to sink in."

Painter nodded again, and they moved off together towards the brighter lit streets of the city center.

"By the way," said Painter as they stepped onto a road lined with colorful, crowded sidewalk cafes, "what did the sub do to deserve the punishment?"

"Doesn't matter. He broke a rule they made together."

Chapter Seven

Brio and the proof of the pudding

Brio was surprised to find Painter in his kitchen when he sloped in from work feeling disgustingly corporate and adult after a day of boring meetings and decisions about stuff he didn't care about. Give him a thirty-six-hour lab session over eight hours of licensing and franchise agreements with lawyers any day.

"Hey," Painter greeted, looking up from the chopping board where he was slicing vegetables. "Hardly ever see you in a suit."

"I avoid them like ebola."

Painter grinned. "But you look so good in them."

Brio was horrified to feel a blush creeping up his cheeks. "Don't get used to it; I'm going to change and take a shower."

"Sit a minute," Painter said. "I need to talk to you."

"I wondered why you were here so early," said Brio, taking a seat at the island unit suspiciously. "Are you feeding me to make up for bad news?"

"No." Painter grinned at him. "I like feeding you. I also like eating what you feed me. It's nice and beats us both eating alone at opposite ends of town."

"'Kay." Brio snagged a slice of avocado from the chopping board. It looked like they were having tacos, and it wasn't even Tuesday.

Painter returned to his chopping. "I'd like to talk about adding some extra rules to our dynamic; I think it's time."

Brio's mood skyrocketed. *Painter wants to stay longer; he wants to give me rules. He thinks I'm worth rules.*

Brio nodded urgently, not daring to speak in case he squeaked, which he would then have to deny. He pulled himself together. "I think that's a very good idea," he said with what he felt was commendable insouciance.

Painter grinned. Already Brio couldn't get much past him.

77

"Do you want to get a notebook, write this down, or we could get Cashel online, have him go through it with us?"

"No need," said Brio, breezily stealing more avocado. "Eidetic memory, I won't forget what you say; I'll get my brain to record it."

"Right," Painter said. "Genius, of course."

"Never forget it." Brio gave him finger guns and then wanted to kill himself.

"You are such a dick." Painter laughed. "But seriously, I'm happy to get Cash online."

Brio considered. "To be honest, this is you and me, it's not the contract, it's not small print – and I have seen a lot of small print today – could we do it, just us, without it being written up in triplicate somewhere?"

"I get you, and I agree with you; let's make this just us."

Painter appeared to gather his thoughts. "I think it's stupid for us to have rules about bedtimes, clothing, kneeling, or stuff like that. I think you and I need to be fluid so I think our rules should revolve around attitude more than anything."

"I like that idea," Brio said, and he did. Past doms and Ash had tried to regulate him via schedules, reporting, and tasks. It hadn't felt right; it felt like cramming him into a shape that didn't fit. This felt like making a space for him, a Brio-shaped space.

"I think the first rule should be about respect," Painter said. "I want you to be respectful to others and to yourself. That includes not putting yourself and others down. And no kink-shaming, Brio, you do that to yourself a lot. It's not good for your soul."

Brio nodded. He knew he did it; he would stop.

"And I know you are brighter than me–"

"I'm brighter than everyone."

"Yeah, and that got you five extra your spanks added to tonight for attitude. But it's going to be a rule that you don't manipulate people or use your intellect to hurt people."

Brio looked at Painter seriously. "Got it. With great power comes great responsibility."

"And that's another five for being a piss-taking little shit; for a bright guy, you don't learn very quickly."

"I'm just so excited we are doing this."

"I know," Painter was indulgent, "and that's why you are getting spanks added not being frog marched to the playroom this minute. But I need you to understand these are serious rules, Brio. I've thought about them, considered them, and manipulation, intellectually, sexually, or emotionally, is a big no as far as I am concerned. "

"I understand," Brio said, "and I'm sorry, I didn't mean to make it seem I wasn't taking them seriously."

"I think we're getting on okay," Painter said. "I think we're making progress, but I would like to make it a rule that if you need something you ask me, if you can, rather than manipulate me into it or bottle it up.

"I think I'm learning your tells, but I'm really new and inexperienced, so making it a rule that you verbalize your needs is going to help us a lot."

"You haven't missed anything so far," Brio said quietly, "and sometimes stuff is hard to say."

"Yeah, I know. I'm pretty sure there's stuff I am never going to be able to ask for, but you have to try. If you're brave enough to ask for it, chances are you're going to get it as a reward – Not guaranteed," Painter added when Brio lit up with glee.

Brio helped Painter clear up the mess from preparing the vegetables, and they kept talking while Painter fried the chicken for the tacos. Brio liked the informal setting, the discussion; it felt so much more natural than previous similar meetings with Doms.

"When I have to take a night off for training, like I did the other night, I need you to call Ash or Richard if there is an issue," Painter said. "I doubt there would be a problem because if I thought you were feeling antsy, I would change my plans, but I'd rather put the protocol in place now so you know what to do."

"I like the way you say protocol." Brio knew he was getting goofy with the way he was looking at Painter. "It's sexy."

"Yeah, protocol is cool," said Painter. "I've been learning it, and I like the idea of running you through positions every day. That feels good in my head."

"We could add it?"

"Let's wait and see. Let's not add too much at once because there is one more important thing I would like to talk about." Painter paused and appeared to gather himself. "I think I'm comfortable progressing sexually."

Brio's heart stood still. *Finally!*

"I can't say when exactly, but I know I was real comfortable making you come; it was lovely. So if things get more intimate between us in the future, I don't want to stop and renegotiate, so can we put it out there now that sex is on the table?"

"Oh, hell yeah." Brio couldn't keep the grin off his face.

Painter laughed. "Not necessarily today or this week, I don't want to put time limits or deadlines on it, but I'm saying, in my head, I'm cool, so we can proceed organically."

"Orgasmically," Brio said.

"You know you're not that funny, right?"

"People think I'm adorable," said Brio with a commendably straight face.

They sat at the island unit to eat their tacos. Brio was hungrier than he thought, and he moaned around a mouthful of soft taco, spicy meat, and creamy guacamole. "God, these are amazing," he said, and Painter grinned.

"So we're clear – no trashing yourself or other people, be respectful, no manipulating, ask for what you want if you can, and Ash and Richard are your safety contacts if I'm not here."

Brio nodded, "What about punishments?"

Painter looked down at his nearly empty plate. "This is the bit I struggle with, the part where I have to fall back on what I've been taught and what I know of you so far. I think time out is pointless for you because you could look at a blank wall for a week and come away with a workable amalgam of specific consciousness theories." Brio raised an impressed eyebrow and Painter glared at him. "And I think chores are just silly, so we're going to have to fall back on corporal punishment."

Brio swallowed, nodded.

"I like the idea of stress positions if appropriate, but I'm less keen on things like kneeling on rice and stuff because if there is pain involved, I want to be the one physically delivering it." Painter's voice had gotten thicker and deeper. "So I think we go for tried and tested impact punishments, spanking, paddles, and canes." He glanced at Brio, and his eyes were dark, the pupils blown wide. With a thrill, Brio realized that this idea aroused Painter. That made it both easier and harder to want to keep to the rules.

"Okay," Brio whispered.

They couldn't seem to look away from each other. Brio was lost in the deep sea blue of Painter's eyes, he felt pulled towards his Dom, and his cock was getting hard in his suit pants. He shifted, and Painter broke eye contact, cleared his throat, and started to clear the table.

"So, is there anything you would like to add to the rules?" Painter asked.

"Uh, yeah." Brio was suddenly shy. He stood and moved to help Painter with the dishes. "If, uh, if we're going to have a sexual aspect to our dynamic, would it be okay if we were monogamous?"

Painter straightened from placing the plates in the dishwasher and turned to Brio. "I'm surprised," he said, "but yeah, that's no problem at all. Monogamy is good; I'd like that."

"Thank you," Brio breathed.

"Come here," Painter said.

With a sigh, Brio slid into his arms. Painter was so tall it made Brio feel small. Painter wrapped his arms around Brio and hugged him gently like he was precious. He put a finger under Brio's chin and tipped it up so Brio looked at him. "Thank you for asking for what you wanted. That was so good of you."

"Reward." Brio didn't even know he had spoken until Painter smiled at him and dipped towards him.

Painter kissed with his whole body, one arm around Brio's waist holding him up, his other hand in Brio's hair, moving him where he wanted him. He curled down and around Brio, and his lips were firm, dry, and wonderful.

Painter tasted of lime and cilantro, spice and heat, and when his tongue pressed against Brio's lips, it was insistent, dominating, and Brio just let go and opened himself to it.

A summer storm threw itself against the ramparts of the mountains, all blue-black skies and grey squalls. Brio lay, morose and irritated, on the sofa in his living room and watched it through the windows. He knew exactly how it felt.

Despite their "talk" and Painter's stated desire to get dirty, animalistic, ugly bumpy, sticky, growly, ya' know, it had been two weeks, and nothing had happened; Painter hadn't got intimate with him. Fuck, Brio hadn't even seen his cock.

He'd felt it - hard and substantial against him when Painter cuddled him after spanking – but of the organ itself, not a sight, not a touch, not a taste, not an orifice explored by it.

It couldn't go on, it really couldn't; Brio was going to explode. Jerking off wasn't working anymore, he couldn't even really be bothered; he just wanted Painter, properly, improperly, any erly.

When Painter said he was ready to go further, Brio assumed, despite Painter's caveat, that he would pounce on him imminently. What a fucking anti-climax that had turned out to be.

Brio flopped over on the sofa, trying to find a more comfortable position. Nothing felt right despite the overlarge, soft, squashiness of the cushions. He needed to fuck.

Painter had been out with his instructor again last night – watching better behaved subs, Brio thought darkly - so Richard and Ash had come for dinner after work and kept him company until bedtime. He hadn't been able to settle after they had left. He knew he should have texted Painter, but sulking seemed a better option, and he had stayed up until the early hours of the morning doing pointless shit and feeling neglected.

Having Ash and Richard babysit him had made his mood even sourer. They were still so goofy in love, and all Brio had was a Venditor Ash had procured for him to make him feel better.

Tears stung his eyes.

He just wanted to know that Painter desired him – no scratch that – he wanted tangible proof that Painter desired him, stiff, hard, erect and coming, tangible proof.

His phoned flashed a warning that the front door had been unlocked. Brio flipped over onto his stomach and feigned an afternoon nap when Painter made his way into the living room.

"Hey." Brio felt Painter's warm hand on his arm. "You okay?"

Brio grunted.

"You tired?"

"Yes." Brio rolled over onto his back.

Painter's ridiculous blue eyes crinkled at the corners as he smiled down at Brio. "You look like a grumpy bear." He bopped Brio on the nose. "Why are you so tired."

"Late night."

"If you couldn't sleep, you could have called me."

Brio blew out a breath, "It was too late."

"What time?"

"Nearly 3 a.m."

"What kept you awake until that time?"

Brio rolled his eyes. "It happens. The problem is that 10.30 p.m. is exactly one minute before 2.30 a.m."

Painter looked thoroughly confused.

"You know how it goes. I looked at the clock at 10.30, and thought, okay, one more game online then bed, but I lost the game and started rambling around the web and saw this link on Pornhub. The next thing I know, it's 2.30 a.m., and I've just beaten off to a dwarf in shibari with a plug up his ass suspended over a guy who gets off from licking his feet."

"Yeah, that happens to me all the time."

"Exactly." Brio hauled himself out of the jaws of comfort that was his sofa. "Want a coffee?"

"Why not," said Painter and followed Brio to the kitchen.

Serving Painter his favorite coffee made the itch inside Brio worse. He ground his teeth; if a tiny service towards his Dom sent him spinning, he needed more. To date, the spankings had helped, the shibari had done more, but long term it wasn't enough. He needed to know that he turned Painter on as much as Painter turned him on. He needed this to be a thing for both of them.

Oh well, Brio thought with his usual shit or bust attitude, time to roll the brat out.

"Ready for your evening routine?" Painter asked politely when they had finished watching an old episode of Buffy – the singing one, Brio loved it; sue him, and that kiss at the end, sexual tension released, so hot.

"Love the euphemism, man," Brio snarked. "Can't we say spanking today?" He pushed a barefoot at Painter's leg, giving him an annoying little kick. "Not man enough to say the S word?"

"Man enough to deliver it," Painter replied evenly.

Brio rolled his eyes/ "I'm not feeling it tonight; I think I'll skip it." He climbed off the sofa and stretched, making sure Painter got a good eyeful of his abs and sharp hip bones when his t-shirt rode up.

"Really." Painter's tone was stony.

"Yeah, think I'll go have a shower, have some me time." He winked at Painter. "Get an early night without a sore ass for a change; it tends to put me off my stroke if you know what I mean."

He strolled towards his bedroom, counting slowly in his head. He got to five before he heard Painter throw himself off the sofa.

Expecting the hand that landed on his shoulder, Brio twirled away and danced out of Painter's reach. "If you want to spank me tonight, sir," he stretched the sir out insultingly, "You are going to have to catch me. Let's see if you're man enough for that."

The responding flash in Painter's dark blue eyes was all the notice Brio had before Painter was after him. The game was on.

Painter didn't say a word as he stalked Brio through the house. He attempted to corner Brio, and when that failed, he aimed for short bursts of speed and lightning-fast grabs, which Brio twisted out of with mocking laughter.

It's like being chased by the Terminator, Brio thought as he took the stairs to the playroom level three at a time, while Painter silently and relentlessly trailed him.

He decided the playroom might have been a mistake as it became apparent that there were far fewer options for escape if Painter cornered him, but his intention had never been to escape forever.

It was still a shock to his system when Painter feinted right, Brio went left, and Painter body-slammed him into the wall. He grunted with the force of Painter's weight. The next second, Painter had his hand around Brio's throat and was hauling him up to look him in the eyes.

"Not in the mood, Brio?" Painter growled. "What a shame."

"Fuck you." Brio figured he must have some sort of death wish because Painter's pupils blew wide, and the hand around his throat tightened. Then Painter was kissing him, biting at his lips, growling. For a moment, it was amazing, and then Painter seemed to realize what he was doing.

"Shit." Painter let Brio go and backed up; he shook his head and rubbed his hands over his face.

No, not happening; that was about to be awesome.

"Hey," Brio whispered, his voice low and careful as he stepped up close enough to Painter that the man could catch him again if he tried. "It's all right. It's only you and me here. There's no one here to judge you."

Painter let out a snort and ran a hand through his hair; he couldn't quite meet Brio's eyes.

"I'm here to judge me," he admitted quietly. "look, what I mean is, I'm not gonna hurt you."

Brio smiled, understanding and just a bit sympathetic, too.

He touched two fingers to Painter's cheek and pressed in. "This is foreplay," he whispered. "We're just playing, yes? To get us both in the mood? I'm not asking you to hurt me. You only need to catch me, and then I'll be all yours, and you can do whatever you want to me. Is that okay? Or do you prefer we get right to the action?"

For a hot moment, Brio could see Painter was tempted to say yes. Except...

You're gonna have to win me. I've waited too long for this; I need the fight.

"Try again?" Painter suggested, he touched Brio's fingers where they rested on his face. "I don't want to give up on the first hurdle."

"There's that fighting spirit," Brio lilted, amused now, and stepped even closer. "I like that. I only have two requests."

"Yeah?" Painter said and swallowed hard.

"Bind me," Brio whispered into Painter's ear. "When you catch me, if you catch me, even if it's just my hands. I need you to do that for me. And when you fuck me..." Painter shuddered when Brio leaned in and touched his cheek with the flick of his tongue. "If you fuck me, if I'm good enough, I need you to fuck me hard."

Yeah, that.

That did it.

Painter lunged for him, but Brio was gone before he could get a solid grip on him.

Brio had always been fast on his feet, and with the adrenalin pumping in his system, he led Painter a chase.

His fatal mistake was underestimating Painter's flexibility and determination. One minute Brio was grinning, feral and taunting, from the other side of the spanking bench, the next Painter had side vaulted over the bench, kicked Brio's feet out from under him, and pinned him to the padded floor.

Painter's larger body pressed Brio into the floor, and his mouth was hot and biting on Brio's neck.

"Oh yeah," Brio gasped as Painter rolled him onto his stomach and held him down with his hips pressed to Brio's buttocks.

"You wanted to be tied?"

"Yeah."

"I'll tie you."

"Go for it, give me what you've got."

Brio nearly swooned when Painted manhandled him to his feet. He should never have underestimated the Dom, he rarely showed his strength, but it was there all right.

"Let's play," Painter's voice was a hoarse growl, and he stripped Brio between bruising kisses.

Within minutes Painter had Brio naked – he hadn't been wearing much anyway – and had walked him back to the spanking bench. Brio felt the hard edge, the cool leather, against his naked ass and moaned in anticipation.

"Color?" Painter held Brio's wrists in one huge hand and a solid grip on his hair with the other, one thick thigh pressed between Brio's.

"Green," Brio moaned and rutted against Painter's thigh.

Painter pressed Brio back onto the bench, and in a single swift movement, slid to the side, pulled Brio's arms over his head, and pushed him up and onto the bench on his back. He manhandled Brio until his head hung over the end and swiftly cuffed his wrists to the legs. Brio felt the blood rush to his head – what blood that hadn't already taken up residence in his groin. Panting heavily, he spread his legs to let Painter cuff his ankles to the other end of the bench.

Watching what Painter was going to do to him would be a struggle in this position, but Brio was pretty sure it would be worth the effort.

When Painter started to undress, Brio's nearly started to cry. Finally, finally, he would see his Dom naked.

Painter, fully naked, all long lines of muscle and tanned skin, strode over to the cupboard and spent a moment selecting what he wanted before he returned with a tube of lube and a slim vibrator.

Brio was being driven mad by the fact that he couldn't get a good long look at Painter's body, the position he was in forced him to hang back over the bench and Painter was, deliberately he felt, keeping out of his direct line of sight to tease his sub.

The first touch of Painter's fingers between his legs made Brio moan. Painter ignored his hard cock and instead used the perfect position he had arranged Brio in to get his fingers working against the rim of Brio's hole.

It turned out that Painter was an evil tease. He moved his finger in and out of Brio's hole with shallow thrusts, occasionally, very occasionally, leaning forward and flicking the crown of Brio's cock with his tongue. Brio sighed and moaned, tugged at his restraints, and wiggled his ass as best he could. He wanted more, but not more for himself, more for Painter. He didn't understand why Painter would pleasure him but not the reverse, that was his job as a sub, and he wanted to do his job.

Painter finally slipped two digits deeper inside Brio, sweeping them round until he located Brio's prostate. Brio arched right up off the bench from the long press of fingers against him.

"That was impressive for being tied up." Painter spoke for the first time, and Brio moaned, doing his best to rock down onto Painter's fingers but getting nowhere. "Now, now," Painter scolded, "Patience. Or at least tell me what you want."

"Want you, sir," Brio moaned throatily and strained to lift his head to see Painter. He was surprised and delighted to see that Painter, standing tall and unashamed at the foot of the bench, was fully hard and that his hand was automatically moving to provide some relieving pressure on his cock.

God, his cock was beautiful. "You're hard, sir," Brio babbled, "You're hard and beautiful."

Painter's cock was in perfect proportion to his lean six foot three frame. Brio had seen a lot of cocks in his time, and they weren't all this perfect, far from it.

Painter was waxed, his groin bare of hair to show off his size and heft. His cock was tanned golden, apart from the head that flushed deep red, and, dear god, it glistened with pre-come.

"It's not for you, Brio," Painter warned as he stroked himself, his face stoic.

"Argh," Brio moaned and let his head fall back. "Sir, please, give me your fingers then. Please touch me again, ple—" His rambling was cut off by another moan as Painter obliged, pushing two fingers inside giving Brio the pressure he needed.

"You like that? That's good because I have more to give you." For a moment, Brio hoped for flesh, but Painter swapped his fingers for the lubed-up vibrator. Turning it on, he angling it so that it rested directly against Brio's prostate.

Brio's cock was rock-hard, and when he flexed his abs and managed another look down his body, he could see it flushed and practically begging for a touch. He rutted his hips as much as he could, but the bindings were secure. Despite Brio's well-known contortionism, he couldn't move far.

He could feel Painter's gaze and when he opened his eyes, Painter was watching him. From the look on his face, he was enjoying the writhing and the sounds that escaped from Brio's mouth.

Brio felt the vibrator slipping from his twitching hole. "Be still," Painter ordered. He reached down and adjusted the vibrator, so it rested tight against Brio's prostate.

Brio shuddered and tried to keep still. Painter rounded the bench towards his head, and Brio's main thought was to get closer to that cock.

Brio's neck and shoulders were killing him; the strain of lifting his head to watch Painter was wearing him out. He let his head fall back for a brief moment as Painter neared him. Licking his lips, he gazed up at the Dom. Painter slid a hand beneath his head, supporting him.

"Is this what you want?" Painter asked as he carefully tipped Brio's head to the side, then, using his free hand, he grasped his cock and brought it closer to Brio's lips.

Brio could smell the hot musk of his body, the salty ocean scent of his precome, the cinnamon notes of his body wash. He stuck his tongue out and strained towards Painter's cock only to whimper softly when he found it out of reach.

The buzzing in his ass was an incessant counterpoint to the flexing of his hole. His body was drenched in sweat, but Brio wanted more. He wanted that beautiful smooth steel silk skin on his tongue and in his throat.

"Please, sir," he begged. "Just one taste; I promise I'll be good."

"Oh baby, what do you want a taste of?" Painter's voice was deeper now, more commanding than Brio had heard before, and his blue eyes glinted. When he let go of his cock it stayed upright, bobbing close to Brio's face, just out of reach.

Brio felt fingers that a moment ago were wrapped around Painter's cock press against his lips. He opened his mouth obediently.

Painter pressed three fingers into his mouth, stretching his lips obscenely. Brio's eyes rolled back in his head at the taste of Painter on his tongue.

Brio took what Painter gave him, breathing through his nose and relaxing his throat as Painter pumped his fingers in and out of his mouth. Between the confirmation that Painter wanted him, the stimulation of his prostate, and the taste of Painter in his mouth, Brio was slipping away to where he needed to be.

"Good boy, such a good boy." Painter pulled his fingers from his mouth. Brio gasped as Painter fisted both hands into Brio's hair. Crouching down, Painter kissed him, his tongue surging into Brio's mouth, his flavor exploded on Brio's taste buds.

"I will take you," he growled into Brio's mouth. "I want to take you, my beautiful boy."

"Please, please," Brio's voice slurred, his body already so close to the edge.

Painter kicked the quick release switch on the cuffs and, reaching down, dragged the vibrator out of Brio's ass. Brio howled at the sensation and the loss.

Painter was between his legs, and Brio's legs were free. Painter hauled him down the bench by his hips until his ass hung over the edge. Brio saw Painter look down, saw the hunger on his face as he lined himself up with Brio's twitching hole, and then he was pressing forward, sliding into him in one long, burning stretch. Fuck he was big, it hurt, but Brio was in heaven, his body impaled on his Dom's cock.

"Oh, god." Brio looked up, and his eyes locked with Painter's. Painter looked wrecked. His mouth hung open, and he panted, the muscles of his shoulders and neck were pumped up, the veins throbbing. With a monumental effort, Painter got himself under control before he hooked an arm under Brio's knee and hefted it up, opening him up more and holding him just where he wanted him.

"Color?" Painter ground out.

"Green, oh god, Painter, green, give it to me."

Painter's hips slammed forward, and Brio screamed in joy.

He could hear Painter, through the pleasure and the pain, praise falling from his lips, "So tight, so good, so beautiful, oh god, Brio, I can't hold it, I can't hold it, please baby, come for me."

Brio came hard, surrounded by the control of Painter, the smell and feel of Painter, but more than that, he came in the knowledge that Painter wanted him, even broken as he was.

"I got you; I got you." Painter's voice was soft in his ear. They were laid out on the soft recovery area of the playroom floor, and Brio was cradled in Painter's arms, being rocked.

Brio blinked up at Painter, his stomach was still covered in his come, and he could feel Painter's come slipping slowly from his aching ass.

"Did I do okay?" he asked.

"You did great; you were perfect!"

Brio smiled goofily up at Painter. "No spanks for me tonight."

"Only if you shut up now."

"Will you sleep with me?" Brio didn't want to ask, but it felt so nice to have Painter's naked skin against his; he wanted a little more of it.

"I'll stay with you until you fall asleep."

Brio pouted. "At least cuddle me." His voice was slipping towards his Little voice; he felt so overwhelmed by his reaction to Painter and Painter's response to him. He needed comfort and was proud of himself for asking for it.

"Okay." Painter leaned down and pressed a kiss to the corner of Brio's mouth. "Because you are a cuddle monster, you get cuddles."

In some far corner of his brain, Brio was aware that Painter had switched modes when Brio required it. The part of his brain that analyzed and made connections noted that for future consideration while the rest of him went offline and gave in to the need for skin to skin contact.

Chapter Eight

Painter and the unfortunate heart

Brio was warm in his arms when Painter awoke. Above them, the glass skylight showed the pearly reds and pinks of dawn. Brio snuffled in his sleep and pressed his face against Painter's chest.

Painter lay there and let self-loathing and joy battle it out in his head and his heart. He remembered the fierce exhilaration of manhandling Brio, catching and pinning him, and then the rush when he flipped him and rutted up against his hard ass.

He smiled; what a brat! Brio had wanted to play. Painter had held back too long, and so Brio - brave, wild, needy Brio, pushed. Painter's hand had strayed to Brio's hair, and he was gently petting it.

Brio had been amazing, so strong, so tough. When Painter had restrained and tormented him, Brio had kept on wanting him, kept asking for him, for his fingers and his cock, whatever Painter was willing to give Brio would have taken.

God, he was so proud of him.

He was less proud of himself. He was unimpressed that it had taken Brio bringing out the brat before he gave in and allowed himself sexual pleasure – it was a pointless denial. After all, he had jerked off night after night to mental images of dominating Brio. All he had achieved with his restraint was to fail to give Brio what he needed and wanted.

He gave himself a minimum pass on how he had handled the scene's restraint and teasing elements. He gave Brio a resounded "A" for how he had responded.

He allowed himself the indulgence of a whole five minutes of remembering the feel of Brio's body around him, the tight heat of his hole, the way it spasmed around him, the look in the man's eyes when Painter had let loose and nailed his prostate. Fuck, Brio had been amazing.

His cock lengthening against his thigh brought Painter back to the present and the biggest issue of all. He looked down at Brio's face on his chest, the half-moon shadows of his lashes on his cheeks, the sleep flush across his high cheekbones, the pout of his lower lip, still swollen from Painter's hard kisses. He sighed and gently maneuvered himself out from under Brio, sliding a pillow in for the man to snuggle against. He knelt beside the bed for a moment, just watching Brio. His heart beat a sad, steady tattoo against his ribs.

Idiot, Painter chastised himself bitterly. He rubbed his hands across his face before bracing them carefully on the side of the bed and standing up. The mattress barely moved and Painter sent up a quick thank you to whoever might be listening above before he tip-toed across the room on silent feet. He made it out of the room without disturbing Brio, who slept on deep and dreamless, sprawled across the bed all dark, messy hair and pale skin luminous in the dawn light.

Painter gathered the clothes strewn around the playroom before he made his way to the bathroom. Once inside, he slumped against the door, wondering what the hell to do now. There was nothing he wanted to do more than crawl back into bed beside Brio. He wanted to wrap his arms around his slim waist and pull him close, to wake him up with soft kisses to the back of his neck and a gentle hand cupping his cock. Like lovers, Painter thought, like two people who could fall in love, not like a Venditor and his Emptor, not like a professional Dom and his sub.

Thoughts like that about Brio were inappropriate; he needed to remember that. It was harder to think, harder to remember when Brio lay next to him, looking innocent and peaceful in his sleep.

Brio, so much contrast wrapped up in one man. Genius and brat, but under it all, so soft, so beautiful and perfect, so full of trust, happy to lay in Painter's arms and... Oh, hell, he had to get his shit together.

Brio didn't want a relationship, Brio wouldn't fall in love, that was clear from the start. Hell, the idea of a connection other than as

Dom and Sub had not formed any part of the contract discussions. This contract was for pure sexual needs – no escorting, no dating, no boyfriend experience required. He would never act as Brio's escort to restaurants or galas, he would never vacation with him, spend holidays with him, do the romance thing that so many Emptores considered a fundamental part of a contract. The best he and Brio could be to each other was friendly; they couldn't even be friends. He needed to remember that.

Painter set about taking a shower and getting dressed. He made it quick, a lick and a promise under the hot water and then made his way to the kitchen to try and get his game face in place before Brio got up. The smartest thing Painter could do at this point was what he had done: get the hell out of that room before Brio woke up.

Keep the boundaries, set the limits, hold the line, Painter reminded himself.

That lasted approximately five minutes after Brio got up and appeared in the kitchen, kitten soft, sweet, and sleep rumpled. Without saying anything, Brio sidled up to Painter and trustingly snuggled into his side. All Painter's good intentions vanished like the steam curling up from his coffee, the coffee he shared with Brio, holding him on his lap and letting him sip from his cup.

It started with a kiss on greeting, a warm press of lips, a little slip of tongue. It progressed to laughing dinners, TV evenings, hot spanking and rough jerk offs that led to late-night cuddles and sleepovers with dopey contented sub in his arms.

This was all on him, Painter decided after the shit hit the fan. It wasn't calculated, it wasn't work, it just evolved that way.

It was a slippery slope, the boyfriend experience with Brio, it all got a bit too domestic too fast with the added frisson of their growing dynamic. It was bound to go wrong.

Painter took his eye off the ball. He forgot, for a little while, that Brio was a complex and demanding Sub with a history he hadn't even begun to scratch the surface of. He let himself pretend he understood Brio; he didn't.

The morning had been perfect. He had woken to Brio's hot mouth around his cock, and he had done what he wanted because he could. He had rolled Brio onto his back, straddled his chest, and fucked lazily into his throat.

It had been wonderful; he had felt so powerful, looking down at that brilliant, beautiful man with his smart mouth stretched obscenely around Painter's cock. He had taken him, taken what he offered. He pressed in deep until Brio choked around his cock, his eyes watering. Without warning, Painter came down his throat, enjoying what his sub offered because it was his right to have it.

He felt amazing afterward, and Brio had been a mewling, wanton, sobbing mess when Painter graciously returned the favor and brought him to orgasm with his mouth while holding his hips down hard enough to bruise.

Brio had been unusually quiet at breakfast as Painter waffled on about the day ahead. He missed Brio's reaction when he announced he would do a solo suspension bondage scene for the first time today.

Painter's pride had been his fatal mistake; he'd wanted Brio to share his excitement because it meant he could suspend him after this. That was what all he'd meant, nothing else.

He pressed a kiss to Brio's forehead before rushing out the door; he didn't remember if Brio replied, he didn't think so.

The minute he entered the house that evening, Painter knew he had made a mistake somewhere along the line. He could feel it in the air, a throbbing, a tension, and he knew this was his fault; he'd done something to trigger what was coming rolling down the path towards him, whatever that may be.

This was his Indiana Jones moment, he'd fucked up with the golden statue, and the boulder was on the move.

He braced himself mentally; he had this, he could do this, he knew it had to happen eventually.

"Did you have a good day at the office?" Brio strolled out of the kitchen wearing a charcoal grey suit and carrying a cup of tea. From the exquisite cut of his tailored jacket to the easy way he held the delicate porcelain cup and the understated elegance of the dark brown leather strap on his Patek wristwatch, he looked like nothing other than out of Painter's league.

Painter was aware that he was too casually dressed, that he had a duffle slung over his shoulder that smelled like gym socks, and he hadn't shaved in three days. This was not how to hold his own with an Emptor.

"How did it go?" Brio's expression was calm, with no edge of snark or bitchiness in his voice. This man wasn't his sub; he was a double doctorate holder who ran a multi-billion dollar company. A man who could neatly slice a human brain while holding a conversation on cognitive resonance, an uber-human, evolved far beyond Painter. This was a man he had never met before.

"It went well," Painter said evenly and carefully placed his duffle on the floor. "Tay was pleased, and the sub said it was an easy suspension; she liked it."

"A female?" Brio quirked an eyebrow. "I didn't know you played with females."

"I wasn't 'playing'; I was training."

"Of course, sorry." Brio sounded anything but sorry. "But shouldn't you be playing with males? Females are anatomically different, after all. The safety protocols would be different, and you're training for males, aren't you? Me, being male, that is."

Painter's mind was moving fast; he needed to get a handle on where this was going, what angle Brio would play. The dominant arching and flexing below his skin, itched to take control and deal with this. Painter wasn't confident enough to let him out, not yet.

"I'm not training to dominate men; I'm training, period. Doing my first suspension on a female sub made sense; they are lighter and more flexible." He stepped up to Brio, letting his height loom over the other man, "But for the record, Brio, I'm pan. I'd 'play' with any gender; I don't give a shit what they have under their clothes."

"How democratic," Brio sneered.

"Sexuality slurs, Brio? You really want to go there?"

"Hardly." Brio's voice was icy. "It is logical for Venditores to be pansexual. The bigger the pool to fish in, the more bucks to bang."

Painter could feel his dominant punching at the door of his control. "You're going to look down on the system that made you a millionaire?"

"I don't work on the practical side of things." Brio's stare was cool, and Painter realized just how different Delphic was for him and Brio.

For Brio, the Agency was a lab full of rats, all fucking and running in his maze and driving themselves mad with pleasure triggers. Painter was one of those rats.

He could practically feel Brio's disdain.

"Yeah, I work on the practical side of things, can't apologize for that." All of a sudden, Painter felt very tired.

"Your parents must be so proud."

Fuck. You had to go there, didn't you? You couldn't just keep the moral high ground; you had to take a low blow.

"Dead, Brio," he said evenly, giving him every chance to end this now.

"That must be a relief," Brio said pleasantly. "Given how much you dislike yourself, it would be even worse if your family saw what you did for a living."

And there it was. The dominant inside Painter threw his hands up in disgust and vanished into the darkness.

Without a word, Painter turned and left. He picked up his duffle and walked out the door. Behind him, there was the faint sound of Brio getting up and walking into the kitchen, the steady, even pace of his step on the floor, unhurried, nonchalant.

Painter leaned against his car and breathed deeply, trying to calm the pain inside. Tay had told him this moment would come, it always did, in all D/S relationships, and he had advised Painter to be prepared for it. And Painter had thought he was prepared, until he wasn't, and his only way of dealing with it was to walk away.

He fumbled his phone out of pocket and thumbed Tay's number.

He closed his eyes and waited, hoping Tay was free.

"What's up, man?" Tay's voice was steady. "Got a feeling this isn't a social call."

"No."

"I take it you met Mr. Emptor, asshole."

"Yeah."

"You okay?"

"Jesus, Tay." Painter shook his head. "He ripped me open in seconds. He knew just where to push. He just sat there, calmly inserted a knife, and twisted it. He didn't even raise his fucking voice."

"No offense, but you're not exactly a complex case. Anyone can see what you struggle with and push at that."

"Still stung," Painter said, "and I still fucked it up, massively."

"What did you do?"

"I walked out."

Tay's sigh was heavy. "You got to get the fuck back in there and punish him, Painter."

"I can't; I'm angry."

"Are you? You don't sound angry to me."

"No," Painter admitted, "I'm not; I'm more hurt and disappointed."

"Why are you hurt?"

"Because I didn't think he thought of me like that; I thought he liked me."

"We could have a whole conversation about why you want him to like you, but that's beside the point. Whatever he said, he didn't mean it; he was pressing your buttons, testing you."

"If I go back in there, I'll hurt him."

"And that's a bad thing in this context, why?"

Painter slowly banged the back of head against the cold metal of the car and blew out a breath.

"Let's take it back to basics," Tay said. "Are you a fair man?"

"Yes, I think so."

"And did Brio break the rules you had agreed upon?"

"Yes."

"Did he know he broke the rules?" Tay's calm run-through of the situation was helping.

"God, yes, he did it on purpose; I just don't know why."

"It doesn't matter why, that's a discussion for later. What you need to know now is that punishment is required under the terms of your agreement and that punishment will be fair because you are a fair man. What do you think he will think if you don't punish him?"

"He will think the rules don't matter to me."

"And do they matter?"

"Fuck yeah, and he matters."

"Then go in there and do it." Tay's voice was implacable. "Trust yourself. Rember, you're a decent person, you always were, and you still are."

"Okay." Painter could hear the confidence creeping back into his voice.

"And Paint, remember, every human interaction is an exercise in power. Work out what power the other person is exerting and stop them doing it, that way, you are in control."

Brio had taken off his jacket and dragged his tie loose; he stood in the kitchen staring aimlessly into the open fridge.

When he heard Painter throw his duffle in the corner, he jumped and turned. His eyes went huge at the look of Painter's face.

"Oh, fuck," he breathed.

"Yeah, oh fuck," said Painter ominously. "Really, really, really, oh fuck."

Brio licked his lips nervously.

"Did you want to carry on with the asshole Emptor routine, or shall we get straight to the result of it?"

Brio straightened his shoulders and said nothing.

Painter could feel his dominant stretching to fill his skin; it felt delicious, like slipping on a well-tailored jacket.

"You can walk downstairs, or I can drag you; the choice is yours," Painter's voice was calm.

Brio didn't say a word; he tilted his head up and quietly walked past Painter towards the stairs to the play suite undoing his shirt buttons as he went.

Chapter Nine

Brio and the pursuit of pain

Painter cuffed Brio's ankles to a spreader bar. "You need this Brio," Painter said, "I need this. We don't shame each other. We don't manipulate each other. We don't play games."

"I'm sorry." Brio hung his head. "You were going on about your training, and I was jealous; I wanted all your firsts in this."

"Well, you are about to get the first punishment I have ever handed out, so congratulations."

Painter pulled Brio's arms behind his back and cuffed his wrists to each other. "Elbows together," he growled. Brio felt the tight pull of the bicep straps Painter wrapped around his upper arms. He swayed as Painter's ministrations pulled him off balance.

"Lean forward." Brio felt the pressure of Painter's hand between his shoulder blades. He bent forward at the waist, Painter holding him by the wrist cuffs.

Fuck, *strappado.*

"Find your balance." Painter grunted as he attached a rope that ran from a ceiling anchor point to the D rings on the wrist cuffs. Brio balanced, the rope to the ceiling had enough give in it that it wouldn't dislocate his shoulders if he fainted or fell and he could go up on his tiptoes to balance out the spread of his legs.

"We need to get this out of the way between us." Painter walked around in front of Brio and grabbed a fist full of his hair, lifting his head so Brio could see himself in the mirror. His legs were spread wide, his arms up behind his back and his flaccid cock was visible hanging between his legs.

"This is punishment," Painter stated, and Brio looked up at him. "This is not revenge, this is not anger, this is leveling the scales, and it is because I want it."

"Yes, sir."

"What is your safeword?"

"Cabbage." Not even the faintest flicker of a smile crossed Painter's face.

"Are you using it?"

"No, sir."

"Twelve strokes of the cane, two of them to your hole."

Brio swallowed, his mouth dry, his heart hammering.

"Then I am going to fuck you."

Brio felt a deep down tightening in his stomach, a fluttering like he wanted to pee. "Sir," he breathed.

"It's going to hurt, Brio; it needs to hurt."

"Yes, sir." Painter was stripping off his clothes, and there was no suggestion that this was an erotic striptease. He unzipped his jeans and pushed them down before he stepped out and kicked them to the side. Fuck, he was already hard, his long cock jerking as he moved.

Brio tried to regulate his breathing as Painter walked over to the cupboard where the canes, floggers, and paddles hung. He could already feel the tension in the back of his thighs from the widespread position. That would increase the pain of any strikes.

He relaxed into the position as much as possible while he could; he arched his back to take the pressure off his thighs and shoulders and pressing his heels into the floor.

"Color?"

Brio watched as Painter strode towards him, a rattan heart cane in his hand. Painter examined it as he moved, his gaze intense as he ran it through his hands to check for weakness; its varnished length glowed red-gold in the light. The sight made Brio speechless with a mix of desire and pride.

"Color?" Painter asked again.

"Green, sir."

"Sure?"

"Yes, sir."

Brio could see Painter in the mirror. His Dom position himself carefully behind and to the side of Brio, then checked the distance between himself and Brio's naked buttocks with the cane, tapping it on Brio's cheeks which caused him to shiver and moan.

"Still, Brio, nice and still." Brio saw Painter stroke his cock lightly with his left hand, and the knowledge that this turned his Dom on sent a deep thrill through him.

There was no warning, no build-up; the first strike landed hard on the lower half of Brio's buttocks. Painter held the cane to the stroke, pressing it into the line. The compressed nerves flared, sending a shockwave of lightening up Brio's back. He yelled, going up on his toes, his back arching against the sting.

"Fuck."

"One." Painter's eyes met Brio's in the mirror as Brio panted through the pain.

Painter pulled back, and Brio couldn't help it; he tensed. The next strike was an explosion of pain as it landed on the sensitive crease between his buttocks and the top of his thighs. He howled, head back, shoulders straining.

"Two."

Brio hung his head, tried to regulate his breathing. *Breathe through the pain, become part of the pain. God, Painter knows how to do this.*

The next strike was just below the first and second, and Brio's balls tightened in fear as the whipping wind of the cane's passage brushed them. The pain radiated through him. He felt it in his buttocks, in his cock, in his spine.

Brio shook his hair out of his eyes and looked up at the mirror. The expression on Painter's face blew him away. Painter's lips shone where he had licked them, and his gaze on the marks he was laying on Brio was intense, greedy.

Painter stepped forward and scratched his nail down the burning lines of the first three strikes. Brio yelled as his nerves convulsed.

"So pretty." Painter's voice was appreciative, possessive. His eyes met Brio's wide-eyed gaze in the mirror.

"Three." he stepped back and again loosely stroked his rock-hard cock, "Color?"

Brio swallowed the saliva in his mouth. "Green, sir," he gritted out, his voice rough in his throat.

"Good boy." Painter smiled at him, and through the pain, Brio felt an answering pulse of pleasure.

Painter delivered the next three strokes in rapid succession. Pull back, land, press the pain in. By the time he paused, Brio was shaking and panting in his bonds.

A far-off part of Brio's brain noted that Painter was perfect at this - varied pace, perfect strikes, and added sensation with the nail scratches over the welts. Brio didn't think he would be able to access that part of his brain for much longer.

The pain was a thrumming song in his skin. When the next two strikes landed parallel to each other further down his thighs, he sobbed through them.

"Stand up, Brio." Painter's hand was on his shoulder, levering him upright and back against Painter's body. He groaned as he straightened. Painter had slackened the wrist rope, and he could lower his arms. He swayed backward, braced against Painter's chest and shoulder. His fingers brushed against the hard length of Painter's erection as Painter wrapped an arm around his waist and held him in place.

"The next two will be across the front of your thighs." Brio groaned, turning his face to the side and sobbing against the hot skin of Painter's throat.

Using his height and reach, Painter leaned around and lined up the next strike. There wasn't as much punch behind it, but the pain was just as severe, shooting up his thigh and pulsing wildly in the root of Brio's flaccid cock.

Brio was crying now, tears streamed from his eyes; he could taste them on his lips. Painter's arm around his waist was like an iron band, a strong lifeline holding him up.

"Oh lovely, look at you, so soft, so good." Painter's voice in his ear was a silken menace.

The last strike across the front of his thighs caused Brio to jerk pathetically in Painter's grasp.

"Good boy, nearly done, soon I will be inside you." Painter pressed a kiss into the sweat-slicked skin of his forehead. "Just two more."

Painter ran his hands up and down Brio's biceps, soothing him and encouraging him to move again.

Everything was so far away now that Brio struggled to move. "Up again, Brio, I need you to bend forward for me, going to do your hole now," Brio waded through the molasses in his mind to move as Painter wanted; his sobs were a slow counterpoint to each movement.

He was aware that the tension was back on his wrists. Obediently he bent forward, leaning into the position.

"Good boy." He smiled through the sobs when Painter praised him.

Looking in the mirror, he could see Painter crouched behind him the cane in an upright position, between the cheeks of his buttocks.

"Lower Brio, I want you wider." Brio dipped lower, arching his back and pushing his ass back towards Painter.

"Gorgeous," said Painter.

Brio saw him pull the tip of the cane back. When he released it a pain fiercer than any he had felt before exploded in his anus. He screamed and convulsed and would have fallen if Painter hadn't been prepared and rose to grasp him around the waist and hold him safe.

The pain wasn't going away; it swelled and swelled and filled Brio's whole body. He had never felt anything like it before.

"Just one more, baby."

Brio realized that through his sobs he was pleading. "Please, please, please, sir."

Painter urged him back into position. Brio went obediently, lowering himself with total submission. Everything but the pain was soft and fuzzy now. The pain was a roaring wind that surrounded and buffeted him, a hurricane that lifted him higher.

The last strike of the cane on his asshole was a shriek of sensation that sang in his head. He sobbed into it, his head hanging low, his sweat-soaked hair stuck to his forehead.

He was distantly aware of Painter's voice and his hands. "Going to take you now, Brio, going to fuck you. Tell me your color, give me your color, baby."

There was cold lube on the burning star of his asshole, and Painter's hands were biting into his hips.

"Green, green, green. Please, sir, green."

Brio screamed, a thin long wailing note when Painter thrust forward brutally into his hole. His body convulsed and then submitted to his master and opened for his cock. Painter groaned and fucked into him again, pushing in deep as he hauled Brio back by his hips.

"Yes, that's it. Oh god, you are so fucking tight."

Painter set a punishing pace, and Brio was nothing more than a collection of nerves firing pain and pleasure through his limbic system.

He was here for Painter; he surrendered himself to Painter. Inside his head, he reveled in enduring what his master chose to give him.

"My boy, my beautiful boy, look at you."

Brio opened his eyes and looked in the mirror. Painter had loosened the wrist rope and had pulled him back against his body. He was a golden god that held Brio in his arms, that bent him and controlled him and made him complete. Brio could see the fierce possessiveness on Painter's face and the drugged joy on his own.

Painter reached around and cupped Brio's flaccid cock, a tender gesture at odds with the harsh thrusts of his cock into Brio's abused ass. "So soft, so pretty, taking it for me."

Brio moaned; he could feel a rising tide low in his belly, not an orgasm but a slow rising of pleasure and pain mingled together. The muscles of his ass tensed, his perineum pulsed with a slow convulsion. He felt like he was overflowing.

He rolled his head back against Painter's chest. "Sir," he whispered through the sunlight of the pain that flooded his body. "Going to, going to–"

He was aware of rippling spasms in his ass and his cock pulsing slowly in Painter's loose grasp as warm wetness spilled out of it and over Painter's hand and ran down his legs.

Painter groaned, and with one last thrust, spilled his come into Brio's clenching ass.

Brio sobbed quietly, empty and far away, washed away by dopamine, blown high into space by cortisol.

Painter's voice was distant, and he strained to hear it. "Fuck, Brio, we're done, that's it. It's over; you're finished, baby."

He tried to pull himself together, to get back to his Dom, something in Painter's voice told him he was needed. He swam through the dark, starry spaces in his head, looking for the way back.

He felt Painter's hands on his body and heard the grunt when Painter picked him up. "Gonna put you here, Brio, talk to me, baby, how are you?"

"Okay. I here," Brio slurred. He blinked heavy eyes at Painter whose face gradually swam into view. "I'm okay, I'm good."

Painter was pulling soft throws over him, arranging a pillow under his head, avoiding his eyes. Brio felt the first prickles of wrong in his soft, black haven.

"I'm going to go call Ash."

"No. Please, no. I'm okay."

Brio couldn't get control of his limbs; they jerked but wouldn't respond to his orders, too soon, too fucking soon. From where he had been laid out on the recovery mat, he saw Painter cross the room and drag his jeans on. He didn't look back as he pulled his t-shirt over his head and ran from the room.

Brio curled tight into himself and waited for Ash, again.

Chapter Ten

Painter and the Submissive's suggestions

"I used to think this place was just for the professionals, but it seems that anyone can just wander in," Painter said.

Richard smiled, crossed the room, and hopped up onto the spanking bench, legs swinging. "You forget I was a Venditor too."

"Yeah, for like fifteen minutes until you found your Happily Ever After."

Richard tilted his head to one side. "I was lucky," he said. "And I know it; I know it every day."

Painter continued to stretch and work the rope through his hands. It had become second nature to care for the rope. The rope felt good, like an extension of himself, a competent and useful extension, not evil, not like the part of him that beat a vulnerable man until he screamed and wet himself.

He clenched his jaw, hard. He wanted to cry, wanted to be sorry, but inside his head, the shadow brother was crowing his victory.

"Do you want to talk about it?" Richard asked.

"Nope." Painter popped the "P" obnoxiously.

"Would it help to know I have done it?"

"Done what?"

"Submissive wetting, male squirting, whatever you want to call it."

Painter stilled and looked at Richard. Normal, nice, Richard, in his plain jeans, white t-shirt, decent haircut, and wedding band.

"You know what happened?"

"Probably better than you do." Richard's voice was gentle.

Painter dropped the rope and hopped up onto the spanking bench next to Richard, their shoulders brushed.

"I hurt him," he said. "I caned him. I fucked him, and at the end, he wet himself."

"That's one way to look at it," Richard said mildly. "Or you could y that you gave him the pain he craved in a controlled environment, en got pleasure from the body he willingly offered you, and he was so ppy, so proud of himself, that he hit a submissive state so profound s pelvic floor muscles contracted involuntarily, his bladder flattened d he had an emission that was a mixture of urine and semen. It's own as male squirting or submissive wetting."

Painter stared at Richard.

Richard shrugged, "I did it once; Ash was so overjoyed he tried to y me a car."

Painter barked out a shocked laugh.

Richard rolled his eyes and grinned. "I know, ridiculous, but he was damn happy about it like I had given him something special."

"I didn't know," Painter said. "I've never heard of such a thing."

"Neither had I," said Richard. "But then there were a lot of things I never heard of before Ash. I looked it up though, because he is not e font of all my knowledge, and yeah, it turns out he was right. Some ily bored scientists in Ohio caught a Doppler scan of a sub having an isode."

Painter shook his head at the crazy in the world.

Richard nodded in apparent agreement. "Yeah, funny old world. it the thing is, it's involuntary; you can't make it happen. It's not like b this place long enough and whoosh.

"It's not just physical; it's everything, brain, body, sense of self, nnection to the dom. It's like when puppies wee on the floor when e Alpha dog looks at them a certain way. It's fear, love, respect, pain, y, safety, all rolled into one."

"Wow," Painter breathed. "That's amazing; you should have let him iy you the car!"

"I probably would have if I remembered a damn thing about it." ichard looked almost wistful. "I was so deep under all I remember is coming around and being wrapped up in his arms, while he smothered me with kisses and wiped me down like I was a gold statue."

They sit in silence for a while before Painter finally said, "I fucked up massively, didn't I?"

"Yeah," Richard said softly. "But we can fix it."

"Where is he?"

"I left them in the Little room."

"Ash stayed with him?"

"Yes, he can't be alone right now."

"I thought he and Ash weren't compatible?"

"They are for aftercare; all good Doms can do aftercare, and Ash is used to doing this for Brio."

Painter hung his head; he wasn't a good Dom. He had left Brio. Ash had called him a fucking pussy asshole when he called him to say he thought Brio was going to drop but couldn't cope with it.

"Ash mad?" he asked.

"Fucking raving," said Richard placidly.

Richard was silent for a moment, head hanging between his shoulders, his eyes on the floor. "Ash asked me once, back in the early days, when the whole submission thing was so new and confusing if I was happy. When I thought about it, I realized that yes, I was. Submission didn't make my problems go away but it did make them seem less overwhelming.

"At the time, my mum had just died, my dad was sick, and things were financially precarious." He looked sideways at Painter and grimaced. "And that's putting it mildly. But when I was with Ash in that one part of my life, there were no worries. Ash was there, in control, taking care of me in this weird way, but taking care of me all the same. Despite all the confusion, it felt freeing, and I was happy.

"I don't think it matters if you are submissive or dominant, that feeling of getting one thing right can spread throughout your life. Like a catalyst, it helps all the others pieces fall into perspective."

Richard raised his head and his kind, dark eyes, soulful and calm, locked with Painter's. "So the thing you have to ask yourself, Painter, is, do you feel happy?"

Painter blinked, breathed, and his eyes prickled with tears. Yeah, he was happy; when Brio was under his hand, he was happy. When Brio looked up at him with adoration and respect, he was happy. When Brio teased and tempted him, then stood pliant and beautiful within his ropes, he was happy, and when Brio took the punishment he gave him, he was beyond happy.

"What do I do now?" he asked.

"Well, I think we coil up these ropes, put them away, and then we go back to Brio's house and see about slotting you into his Little scene and we'll play it by ear."

"Should I see him now?" Painter asked. "He's in a drop."

"Then you can bring him back up," Richard said with sweet confidence.

Painter could hear Brio before he saw him. "I like Archaeopteryx," Brio said in the voice of a child, young and opinionated. "I like the way it sounds in my mouth like I can taste the word." He giggled. "And I like the idea that it's a transition between dinosaur and bird." Brio was a genius. and this was him as a child, prodigious and precocious. "I think the transitions between one state and another are more important than the states themselves."

Painter stepped closer to the open door and peered inside. Ash lay on his stomach on the playroom floor, his head pillowed on his folded arms. Brio sat cross-legged on the floor beside him, arranging dinosaurs up and down Ash's spine and across his shoulders.

"What do you think, Ash?" Brio carefully placed a small velociraptor between Ash's shoulder blades.

Ash didn't have time to reply before Brio looked up and saw Painter in the doorway, his huge dark eyes looked stricken and his arms jerked. "Painter," he breathed, and there was such yearning in that tone that Painter wanted to weep.

"Hey, baby boy." Painter hoisted a smile onto his face. Ash turned his head to look at him and huffed out a snort before turning back as if he couldn't bear to look at Painter.

Painter stepped carefully into the room, Richard close behind him. Brio didn't take his eyes off Painter.

"Can I play too?" Painter asked quietly.

Brio looked down and bit his lip. "Yeah," he said softly, "If ya want to."

"Good," Ash pushed himself up from the floor, scattering dinosaurs. "I think we were about to re-enact the Chicxulub impact, and I have a feeling it was going to be on my bottom!"

He squatted and rubbed noses with Brio, making him giggle. "Will you be okay to stay here with Painter? Ricky and I are going to go and make something to eat."

"Yeah," Brio ducked his head, shy again.

"Good." Ash hopped to his feet and stepped into Painter's space; they were nearly the same height, Ash just an inch shorter.

"Nice to see you, Painter." Ash's tone was mild, but the look in his eyes, hidden from Brio, was pure loathing. Shame rushed through Painter, and he felt a flush rise in his cheeks. He looked away, said nothing.

Ash stamped out of the room. Richard rolled his eyes, grinned at Brio, and then followed him.

"Ash is cross," Brio said quietly. He was wearing old sweatpants and an ancient t-shirt with "My Attitude isn't Bad, It's in Beta" written on it. His hands twisted the hem of the t-shirt, stretching it out.

"I think Ash has a right to be cross," Painter said as he sat on the floor opposite Brio and began to drag the scattered dinosaurs towards him.

"Are you cross?" Brio asked carefully.

"No," Painter looked at him, "I'm sorry."

"I'm sorry too," whispered Brio, his eyes filling tears.

"You have nothing to be sorry for," Painter said firmly. "I was the one who did something wrong."

Brio looked dubious and chewed his lip.

It was weird, Painter found it easy to see the child rather than the man in front of him. Brio wasn't small, and while he was flippant, snarky, and frequently playful, it was an adult playing. This was no adult, this was a child, and Painter felt a fierce protectiveness fill him.

He didn't know why Brio chose to regress like this, but like with everything about Brio, there were layers upon layers, and it would take years to peel them all back and kiss the insides. He wished he would have the time to do that.

"Can I read you a story?" he asked.

Brio smiled at him from under his messy hair. "Yeah, that would be cool."

"Okay, go pick a book."

Painter got up, went over to the daybed, and arranged the pillows into a nest against the wall. Kicking off his boots, he climbed up and settled back.

"Come here," he said to Brio, who had selected a book from the crammed shelf.

Brio scrambled onto the bed and clumsily scooted himself between Painter's spread legs. Painter pulled him back against him and nuzzled into his hair. "Good boy," he said.

Brio smelled of sweat and tears, but underneath was the faint odor of come and lube. Painter hugged him and felt like the biggest shit on the planet.

"We'll read this, and then we'll have a bath, okay?"

"Yeah." Brio snuggled back him. "Can I have bubbles?"

"Of course you can."

"I like bubbles. Their surface tension balances the outward force due to the pressure difference between the inside and the outside air; it's a neat trick."

Sometimes Painter thought Brio was trying to explain something to him, but he just wasn't quite getting it.

Painter nearly left again when he stripped Brio for his bath and saw the welts on his body, eight on the cheeks of ass, and two across his thighs.

He was on his knees before Brio, easing his pants down, and Brio hissed as the fabric pulled across his thighs.

"Shit, I'm sorry baby, I'm sorry."

He looked up at Brio and their eyes locked. Brio was slowly coming up from his Little space, and when he spoke his voice was more mature. "Don't be sorry," he said, "I like them. I know that's weird, but I like to feel them and touch them."

Painter softly placed his palm over the welt on the front of Brio's left thigh. He could feel the heat in it, the swollen ridge. Above him, Brio sighed.

Painter made sure the water in the bath was only lukewarm. and even though he helped Brio ease into the bubbles. the sub still hissed with pain.

Eventually, the tension started to ease from Brio's muscles, and he relaxed back into the water with a sigh. "That's so much better," he said.

Kneeling by the side of the tub, Painter ran his hand up and down Brio's wet arm, gentle strokes, keeping contact. "Can I wash you?"

Brio looked at him with a sweet smile. "That would be lovely."

Painter took his time; he massaged sweet shampoo into Brio's thick dark hair, rubbing his scalp in light circles until Brio moaned with pleasure. He held Brio's head back, shielded his eyes and rinsed the soap out before picking the softest sponge he could find. Sitting on the side of the bath, he began to wash Brio's limbs with long slow strokes.

By the end of it, Brio was dopey and doe-eyed, yawning and pliant. Painter helped him out of the tub and gently patted him dry. Brio stood silent and still when Painter gently dressed his welts with numbing cream and carefully applied arnica cream to his hole. His anus was swollen and bruised, but there was no tearing. He moaned softly when Painter rubbed in the cream.

When they got upstairs, Ash and Richard had disappeared, leaving a pot of tomato soup on the stove and grilled cheese sandwiches in the warming oven along with a note telling them to get some sleep.

Brio sat quietly on a seat at the island, and Painter fed him small bites of sandwich dipped in the soup. Brio never took his eyes off him, and every few minutes, Painter felt compelled to touch him, brush his hair off his forehead, trace the shell of his ear, wipe a crumb from his plump lips with a thumb.

"Can I sleep with you?" he asked eventually.

Brio nodded.

He half-carried Brio to his room, the man yawning and stumbling as exhaustion finally caught up with him.

As he climbed into bed with Brio, Painter realized that this was the first time he had slept in this room; previously, he and Brio has stayed in the bedroom attached to the play suite. He wondered if he should have taken Brio back there, but it was too late now.

Brio was curled into his usual question mark position on his side, and Painter pressed up against him, bare chest to Brio's warm back. Their legs were tangled together, and Brio was already breathing steadily as he drifted to sleep.

Painter pressed a kiss to the back of Brio's neck. He smelled like clean skin and body wash, warm summer air, and spearmint toothpaste. He wanted to say something profound, something to send Brio into sleep, how important he was, how much Painter thought of him, admired him, adored him.

He didn't dare start to speak; he didn't know where he would stop. Instead, he just held Brio close and breathed him in.

Chapter Eleven

Brio and the workday routine

Brio could pretend; he could pretend the drop never happened. He could sink into the moment because he was a world-class ostrich with his head so deep in the sand that he could smell lava.

So he snarked and teased, grumbled when Painter bent him over to spank him, but he remained a good boy within the rules. He kissed and flirted and worked at being himself until it was routine again. He planned to be himself for as long as possible.

"What ya doing?" Brio asked, opening the fridge and scanning it as if expecting snacks to be handed to him.

Painter was leaning back precariously on the stool by the island, his boots up on the polished black granite. "Online shopping," he said, scanning through his phone.

"Are you buying me sex toys and slutty lingerie? Because I will be very impressed if you did."

Painter was off the stool and pressed up against Brio's back in a heartbeat. "Would you wear slutty lingerie if I asked you to? Or would you rather that I did?"

"Oh, god," Brio's voice dropped, broken, and the drink he had just taken from the fridge hit the floor.

"Is that oh god, yes you, or oh god, yes me?"

"Both, definitely both. Maybe even at the same time, but yeah, either, or." Brio turned into Painter's embrace, cupped his hands on either side of Painter's face, and drew him in for a kiss that went from tender and sweet to biting and deep with his legs around Painter's waist, being dry-humped against the fridge within minutes.

"Would it make your boring days better to wear something silky and slutty under that business suit you hate so much?" Painter growled into Brio's ear. Brio's cock grew hard against Painter's body.

"Can you exercise that beautiful brain of yours knowing that when you get home, I'm going to strip you down, and it will just be me and you and black lace that smells like your cock. Do you think you'd be able to get anything done when all you can think about all day is how I'm going to play with you later in your pretty panties?"

Brio groaned and rubbed himself against Painter. "Please, please, let's do that, can we do that? I want to sit in meetings and feel my cock leaking in my panties."

Painter bit at Brio's neck. "Oh. hell yes, we're going to do that, and the toughest decision I will have to make is, do I suck you off through the silk, or do I pull them to one side and fuck you?"

Brio knew he was in trouble; it was 2 a.m., and he should have been home eight hours ago. He'd lost time, slid down the rabbit hole of research, and now here he was, sneaking into his own house.

Painter was on the sofa watching TV, laid out long and lithe with his arm tucked behind his head. "Hey sweetheart," he said when Brio slunk into the room.

"Can we just get to the part where you're mad at me and get it over with," Brio burst out.

"You think I'm mad, or do you think I ought to be mad?"

"Yes," replied Brio, who even this tired could still exercise logical thought.

"I'm not," Painter said.

"But I'm supposed to be home by six, and you were waiting. For eight hours!"

"Come here."

Brio went reluctantly, and Painter pulled him down onto the sofa beside him and pressed a kiss to his forehead.

"When we agreed on the contract, I think I was aware that you are an important scientist who co-runs a multi-billion dollar organization, and as such, while you might have promised to always be home by six, I didn't think you could always manage that. Did you mean that promise?"

Painter propped himself up on one elbow and ran his fingers through Brio's hair, which felt really nice. He hesitated to press back into it, but oh, god, it felt good.

"I probably meant to keep it, but I think, like you, I figured that I probably wouldn't be able to manage it?" Brio found himself saying with surprising honesty.

"Are you, or are you not, an adult?"

"Chronologically, or–"

"Brio!"

"Yes, I am," Brio said, "but you know, rules and boundaries and..."

"Your psych report says that your tendency to overwork can exacerbate your issues," Painter said. "But you're... look, you're a genius Brio, the work you do is important, and I don't think it is up to me to tell you when you have to stop unless I see a prolonged downward trend and even then, fuck, you pay me for this, and I think there are other ways to keep you balanced.

"If you want to stay up all night and go to sleep drooling on your graphs, that's up to you; I'm here to give you what you need, not babysit your entire life."

It wasn't even the first time Painter had told him things like this. According to Painter, the rules he and Brio made between themselves were more important than the contract from Delphic. Brio sighed. Some things were hard to get his head around. He expected to be a fuckup, and he expected Painter to be angry about that, but this sort of thing never made Painter mad; it just made him want to take care of Brio.

Painter was kinda perfect like that.

Brio kept waiting for the other shoe to drop, and there didn't seem to be one.

"Sometimes I think you should," Brio said.

"What, be mad at you?"

"Yeah."

"Not gonna happen, baby," Painter said. "'Because you don't really want that, that's too easy, it's a cover for what you really want, and I'm not going to do it.

"I've got my head around hurting you when you need it, and I can justify it, but I can't get my head around yelling at you like a child. That will just piss you off and irritate me. Trust me; I'm here to figure out what you need."

"I do trust you."

"Liar," Painter said without malice, burying his nose in Brio's hair.

"You don't think enforcing boundaries would be good for me, maybe reinforced with a solid punishment?" Brio asked, and there was that uncertainty in his voice again. His brain was trying to work its way through the maze of what he wanted, what he needed, and what he absolutely didn't want to ask for.

"I think you want some pain," Painter said, "but you're not getting flogged or spanked, Brio, not as punishment for making your own decisions. That's a hard limit."

"I'd get it because I need it and want it, and you want to give it to me?"

"That's right," Painter said.

I love you, Brio thought, but he didn't say it because it was the last thing he had, and he was saving it for when it was needed most.

"Let's get some sleep, baby," Painter told him. "We can play tomorrow, whatever way you need."

In bed, Brio snuggled into Painter's heat, drawing it around himself like a blanket. He kept pushing the line, and Painter never pushed back the way he expected.

Maybe there wasn't a line; perhaps there was just the two of them, both with complex needs, somehow spinning together in revolutions that were slowly syncing.

Brio wasn't sure if that made things better or worse.

Brio was naked. Painter had strung him up by his wrists from the suspension ring and was circling him, predatory and intense, with his favorite flogger draped over his shoulder.

Brio could smell the heady leather scent of the flogger, and his body already tingled where Painter had warmed him up with it. They both loved that flogger, it looked amazing in Painter's hands, and nothing said high class, high maintenance slut like a handmade heavy elk flogger. All thud no sting; it was like being flogged with a velvet curtain.

"Tell me what you want," Painter encouraged, "and if you give enough detail, I'll think about letting you have it."

"I want... want to strip you out of those clothes. I want to... I want you to let me please you. I want to taste you, lick you all over, blow you until you're weak with it, and then I want to ride you."

"More detail."

"I want to kneel before you, lick up the inside of your thighs, bury my nose in the crease of your groin – I love your scent there, I could breathe it in forever. I want to lap at your balls, suck them gently, so gently, roll them with my tongue."

Painter pulled the flogger from his shoulder. His wrists, expert and pliant, rotated easily. The thick falls of the elk skin were a high flying flag-waving instrument of pleasure in his grip. The thud of it across his back had Brio moaning with pleasure.

"More, tell me more," said Painter, and Brio struggled to bring his brain online along with his mouth and tell him.

"I want to ride you. I never get to ride you. I want to do all the work. I want you to lie there while I take your cock in my ass with one long slide. It'll burn, but I don't care. I want you to be able to lie there and let me sweat over you.

"It's going to hurt so good because you are so thick, and I love the feeling of you stretching me." Brio was babbling now, wanton and desperate. "I want to grind myself on you, twist my hips and feel you nailing my prostate. I want to come on you and then lick it off, bathe you with my tongue. Oh, please, Painter, let me."

Painter and I, we're two different kinds of extreme, thought Brio, both unconventional, working within our natures as best we can.

Brio was hard-edged and soft-centered. Painter was soft-shelled over the soul of a sadist.

In the playroom, shielded against the world, hiding from everyone else but visible to each other, here, inside the contract, where the algorithm placed them, they worked.

I want this to keep on working; please let me be almost loved a little longer.

Painter let him down, and they were on the floor. Brio lost himself in the push and pull of Painter's body. Painter, the expert Venditor, could almost effortlessly undress, sliding and maneuvering around so that as much of that sleek, bare skin as possible kept touching Brio's.

Painter never seemed to get his shoe caught up in the leg of those sinfully tight jeans. Painter could tug his shirt over his head one-handed, and the resultant fall of his hair looked sexy, not merely messy.

Soon enough, he had that perfect body bare, exposed, and Brio was too busy worshiping every inch of it to worry about his own needs. He had this, he could have this, and there was nothing that Brio wanted more.

Brio watched Painter as he stood out on the terrace, in the morning sun, with his coffee and multihued hair and the snow on the mountains in the distance.

He knew the shoe was going to drop; it was just a question of when. He took everything he could get because he could feel it coming, the end drawing near. He needed to stockpile the memories, the sensations, the ecstasy, for whatever the future would bring.

Chapter Twelve

Painter and the long dark tea-time of the soul

After his evening spanking, Brio would be relaxed and docile. Tha was when Painter liked to explore him, laid out on the bed or the playroom floor, supple, soft, and yielding.

Painter loved the color of Brio's hole. Genitals are unique to each human, and Painter had played with pale wraith women whose genital blushed a dark rose and olive-skinned men whose cockheads were wan and ghostlike.

Brio's hole was a few shades darker than the rest of his skin and wa like a target for Painter to zero his tongue into. He loved the shadow dip of it and the dark tan rim, and if he opened it up, the inside woulc be red and gleaming.

On nights like these, he wanted to open Brio up until he coulc see right inside to the molten core of him and then take it. His mouth flooded with saliva, his cock twitched, and he knew he wanted Brio in every way possible, and he knew he could take him in every way possible because Brio would let him.

And more than that, he knew that he loved all Brio's parts and what they do together. He loved the care he is allowed to give him, the pair he can inflict, and the control he has over him.

He came to this contract reluctantly, accepted his dominant side reluctantly. He found delight in inflicting pain reluctantly, but nothing had been as reluctant as admitting to himself that he loved Brio.

Maybe he could get over it, learn to live with it, and hope that it faded in time. It seemed unlikely, given the dynamic.

His hands were cool on the hot cheeks of Brio's freshly spanked ass He spread them slowly and dabbed again at the star of his hole with his tongue. Brio sighed languorous and low, and Painter never wanted to let him go.

Winter was coming. Snowstorms would soon sweep down on the city and nobody cared but Brio who was morose at summer's end.

Painter found Brio in the kitchen one morning, his head on his folded arms, staring intently at a soap bubble that had floated free from the washing up and now rested on the granite worktop, it's surface tension oily and roiling.

Painter pressed a kiss to Brio's head. "You okay, baby boy?"

Brio puffed out a breath, and the bubble popped. "I've got something stuck in my head; it's annoying me."

Painter ran a hand through Brio's hair, petting him lightly. "What?"

Brio didn't make eye contact, just stared into the middle distance, "I read a quote from this old designer guy, some big old queen, from decades ago. He said, 'I personally only like to bed high-class escorts. I don't like sleeping with people I really love. I don't want to sleep with them because sex cannot last, but affection can last forever.'"

There was nothing Painter could possibly say to that. On so many levels, it would be the death of him.

Brio looked at Painter, his expression haunted. "On the good days, I know it's not true, of course, it isn't. But on the worst days, the really bad days, I think it might be the best I'm ever going to get."

Brio breaks Painter's heart in so many ways.

That was the day Painter went to speak to Cashel.

Painter looked down at Brio, a slight smile on his face, peace in his heart. Brio knelt between Painter's spread legs, naked, his hands crossed neatly behind his back. His mouth was warm and wet around Painter's soft cock, his cheek rested on Painter's thigh. His big brown eyes, hazy with his submission, blinked slowly as he looked up at Painter.

"My beautiful boy." Painter used a finger to wipe the drool from the edges of Brio's swollen, flushed lips. "That's lovely, just hold it there, no sucking, just hold it, keep it warm."

Painter could feel the slow calm cycling of Brio's brain, the serenity that radiated from him, the usual storm of his energy lulled into easy rolling waves.

They both floated on the same sea.

Painter ran a hand through Brio's hair, allowed himself to put all his love into the touch, said the words in his head, kept his mouth shut.

The next day he told Brio he was leaving.

"I'm quitting, Brio," he said. "Turns out I am a sadist, but I'm not a total bastard."

Brio looked at him steadily.

"I can't do this for money. I could fuck for money because it wasn't me, but this is me, I've accepted that, and for me, part of that means not getting paid to touch you the way you need." He shrugged. "It seems somewhere along the way I developed integrity along with a firm right hand."

Brio obliged him by quirking a smile. "What are you going to do instead?"

Painter blew out a breath and dropped his gaze. "I spoke to the agency; I'm going into training at Delphic. It turns out that if you put

lot of mileage on a guy real quick, along with Tay's mentoring, means
'd make a passable instructor. That, and my charming personality.

"Cash thinks my previous self-doubts give me a healthy angle on
he whole thing. I bring an extra level of safety to the process, which can
nly be a good thing. People like me shouldn't be allowed out without
afeguards."

Brio briefly rested his hand on Painter's arm. "You're not so bad,
ou know."

"No? It seems I have more honor than I thought which is a rare tick
1 the plus column of a very shitty personality analysis."

Brio's voice was steady, but his eyes were shadowed with pain.
ainter could feel him starting to build the walls up, brick by brick.
oon he wouldn't be able to feel him at all.

"Will you be dominating the subs at Delphic?" Brio asked.

"Yeah, I have to, it's part of the role, but I've said I have a hard limit
f no sexual components when I'm training."

Brio seemed relieved at that. Painter guessed he had a point; the
lea of him bouncing out the door and taking on a whole line of subs
ould have been too close to Brio's issues.

"What do you think I should do?" asked Brio.

"Be happy because you're amazing." He just couldn't think of
1ything else to say; he couldn't bring himself to suggest Brio find
meone else.

"Yeah, not so helpful, never could get on board with that."

"I'm sorry, Brio, I just can't do this with you for money. It's wrong
r me." He took a deep breath and looked deep into Brio's eyes. "I've
ver had control of anything before this. I never wanted control of
1ything before this. Control required effort. I just slid through life,
king the line of least resistance, going with the flow.

"Turns out, once I got a little control, I wanted all the control. You
ve me control of you, and that gave me control over me. That's a good

thing, and I can't tell you how grateful I am for that. But that's why
quit."

"I understand."

Painter looked at him. "Thank you for being so cool about this.
thought you'd go nuts."

"You do know my other doctorate is in psychology?"

"I forgot," Painter said, "I'm only human, but yeah, figures. So
you're going to be okay." He made it a statement, not a question, an
put as much of his newly minted dominance into it as he could. "You'v
got friends. You've got people who love you, and you have peop
watching over you. You'll just keep on being amazing."

"I'll be sad," Brio said.

Won't we all, thought Painter.

Chapter Thirteen

Brio and the promises you keep

And Brio was sad. But sad was okay, sad served a purpose, sad was manageable. Sad wasn't dropping, and it didn't lead to episodes of sexual degradation.

He endured it through the winter because privation and suffering were character building. Although, Brio suspected that he already had rather more character than was strictly required.

He worked with Ash, the two of them noodling away at the algorithm; they couldn't get the switch component to mesh within the submissive, dominant lattices. He needed more data, and then he would fix it. Being snotty, Ash said switches didn't matter; they were by their very definition more balanced and they were boring.

Brio didn't agree, switches were fascinating. He had the feeling that they were the real key to it all. Once he got switches sorted, the whole puzzle would fall open before him like a great big glorious maze, all his to explore.

He hung out with Richard. They went for lunch, and Brio ordered a pineapple smoothy every time because ya never know, even though he did know, but hope, eternal, springing, sort of thing.

Every week he met with Cashel, far from the Delphic offices, in his professional capacity. Brio was a psychologist. He understood the value of therapy, and expected to be in therapy of one form or another for the rest of his life. Cashel listened to all the things Brio couldn't tell anyone else and Brio joked about how paying people to listen to him was his new normal. Cash never laughed at those jokes.

He researched, learned, and laughed – sometimes – and he proved stuff because scientists have to prove stuff.

If you don't prove it, it isn't real.

Brio had promised himself he would tell Painter he loved him when he left him. If Brio knew one thing, it's that breaking promises to yourself is just stupid, and he has never, ever, been stupid.

Late maybe, nervous definitely, but not stupid.

Painter had his own training studio now at Delphic, specializing in ropework. It turned out that when he had nothing else to master, Painter mastered rope.

Brio let himself into the studio early one March morning, unannounced, unexpected, determined.

Painter's studio was huge; rigging, lights, stainless steel track were fixed to the ceiling. Wooden bars filled one end wall, and coils of rope, in all shades and consistencies, hung in neat rows in a rope locker that was at least twenty feet long. Of the man himself, there was no sign.

The floor was padded, the spring light slanting into the room was defused by gauzy curtains. Music played in the background. Soft and slow, hypnotic, sweet music. A dungeon this was not.

At the far end of the room, a construction of intricately woven ropework hung from a square rig.

Brio glided towards it, feet silent on the floor.

He tilted his head to one side, considering, examining. *A bubble?* Constructed as elegantly as a weaver bird's nest, it hung from a single plaited line but was stabilized by guy ropes to the corners that anchored it in place, anchored it in space.

How very beautiful. How very Painter.

"Hey."

Brio turned at Painter's quiet vocalization. He hadn't heard him enter the room.

"Hey," Brio replied, quiet, suddenly shy. He tucked his hands into his pockets, feeling overdressed in his business suit compared to Painter with his bare feet, soft pants, and plain t-shirt.

Painter's scruff was thicker; it made him look more mature. His hair was longer too, winter dark at the roots, summer bleached at the ends. He looked altogether delicious.

Painter stepped a little closer. "It's good to see you," he said. "I missed you."

"Yeah, me too." Brio couldn't look at him yet; the energy was too overwhelming. "I didn't want to come by and see you until you were settled." He indicated the studio. "This is awesome." He waved at the sculptural ropework. "And that, fuck, that is just amazing."

"Yeah, I really got into the ropework; turns out I'm a bit arty!"

"Who knew!"

"Not me!"

They both laughed.

"It's a bubble," Painter said.

"I guessed. It's so beautiful."

"I hoped you would get to see it one day."

"I'm glad I did."

Silence fell between them. A baited breathing space, while their energy swelled around them.

"So, how have you been?" Painter asked eventually.

"Good." Brio managed to raise his head and look him in the eye, briefly. "No orgies, no arrests, no lasting damage."

"No lasting damage?" Painter's voice dropped dangerously low, and his expression turned dark.

"Only my heart."

Painter looked at him steadily.

"And I'm trying to fix that."

Brio knew Painter, knew him with every facet of his multiple, complex personality. He could feel him, even now, after all these months.

Painter swallowed and his jaw was tight; his hands were deep in his pockets. Brio knew what Painter wanted to do with his hands; he wanted to claim, tie, hold, take ownership, and control because it was all about control.

"I love you," Brio said. "Just you. Me, not so much, but you, I love. Please come back to me, for free, forever."

Epilogue

Cashel and the risks worth taking

Painter kissed Brio carefully and with purpose. "I love you," he said. "Thank you for letting me hurt you in the way I need to."

Brio's gaze was steady and calm. He had eyes for nothing but Painter. "You are my world," he said. "Thank you for letting me be what you need."

Cashel felt tears prick his eyes, and he blinked them away rapidly.

Painter moved around Brio slowly and with intent, weaving the ropes around Brio's elegant length, touching and talking quietly to him as he moved. Brio was pliant, doe-eyed, and docile, only his head tilting to catch his Dom's words of instruction and praise.

Birch pressed against Cash's side, together they watched silently as Painter drew Brio up into suspension, floating him within the ropework bubble they shared.

When Painter turned Brio upside down and started to cut him out of his clothes, Tay touch him lightly on the shoulder, making him jump.

"Demo part is over guys. Time to leave them to it," he said, quiet and firm.

Cashel nodded. Silently, he and Birch followed Tay from the studio.

"That was intense!" Birch's voice was quiet, and he sighed. "The connection between them is beautiful but overwhelming."

"Yeah."

Cash leaned against the wall and watched as Tay assessed Birch. "They are intense," Tay said, "but then we specialize in intense, don't we?"

Birch nodded and hung his head. "I'm so glad they made it."

"It was touch and go there for a while there," admitted Cash.

"It doesn't always work out," Tay said gently, "but sometimes you have to take the risk."

"Well, you take the risks," Cash said. "I just get to watch you tak
them."

"Who will watch the watchers?" asked Birch, then he grinned. "
heard that on Star Trek." Tay reached out and ruffled his short hai
laughing at him.

From behind the closed studio door, Brio cried out in ecstasy,
sound so joyous, so free, so pure it made Cash's throat dry. That was
risk well taken, he thought, with no small amount of envy.

The next book in the series is Paid to be Shared

More About Romilly King

Hi, I hope you enjoyed this book. If you did you may want to check out my other novels (and assorted freebies) by visiting my website. All books can be bought direct, at a discount, on my website as well as through all good online retailers.

Romilly King Website[1]

Thanks for reading!
   Rom

---

1. http://www.romillyking.com

Lightning Source UK Ltd.
Milton Keynes UK
UKHW011011070223
416609UK00006B/1607

9 798215 471544